Ordained Footsteps

Steps of The Righteous

Author

DeiAdra NiCoLe

DEIADRA NICOLE asserts the moral right to be identified as the author of this work.

Copyright © 2023

All rights reserved. No part of this publication may be reproduced, stored, or transmitted in any form or by any means, electronic, mechanical, photocopying, recording, scanning, or otherwise, without written permission from the publisher. It is illegal to copy this book, post it to a website, or distribute it by any other means without permission.

Printed in the United States of America.

E-book: ISBN: 979-8-9877100-3-6

Paperback: ISBN: 979-8-9877100-4-3

Hardback: ISBN: 979-8-9877100-5-0

This novel is entirely a work of fiction. The names, characters, and incidents portrayed in it are the work of the author's imagination. Any resemblance to actual persons, living or dead, events or localities is entirely coincidental.

ACKNOWLEDGMENTS

In honor of my Lord and Savior, who is the head of my life, I give thanks. He could have chosen anyone but instead entrusted me to complete this assignment. It is only because of his grace and mercy that this book was possible. I have faced many obstacles along the way, but God is still faithful through it all. God would not allow me to give up, just as he has not allowed me to give up in life. It was out of obedience that this short-story book was published. Obedience is better than sacrifice. Additionally, I would like to thank my children (Darriel and David) for their prayers and words of encouragement. I would like to give a very special thanks to Pastor Linderia Watts-Mobley, who unknowingly inspired the short story "Talitha cumi." Lastly, I would like to thank everyone who supported me. I am forever in debt to you guys. Thank you.

TABLE OF CONTENTS

Contents

INTRODUCTION

This fictional novel highlights literary works designed to entertain, encourage, and, most importantly, give praise while saving lives. However, this book may not be intended for everyone, only a select few, as it touches on religion and religious beliefs. If you're a person dealing with substance abuse, struggling with depression or anxiety, or who has simply given up in life, then this book is for you.

"Ordained Footsteps" contains a series of short stories where each character revisits past events. Events that significantly impact each character's life prompting them to make life changes. The group collectively are all members of the same church where they planned a weekend getaway. The group decided to go hiking to test their survival skills. In many instances, they felt they had all been sheltered and wanted to know if they had what it took to survive solely off the land. After a long day of hiking, the group ultimately comes together, where they all sit around a campfire sharing their life stories. In sharing their life stories, they will share the trials and tribulations they endured before dedicating their lives to Christ. Each short story is fitting of its titles as each speaks for itself.

In our first short story, "Talitha Cumi," you will be intrigued to learn the life story of the beautiful and talented Phoebe Westbrook. Phoebe is the church's minister of music, where she not only composes music but is a skilled performer and directs the choir. Immediately following the second short story, just as its name implies, "Lord, have Mercy," you will be introduced to none other than God's gift to mankind and hopeless romantic, Mercy St. James. Mercy is the choreographer for the church's praise dance ministry. Third, you will be introduced in "God Decides" to Ronald and Chinaka Henderson-Babette if trouble is to be found, she will indeed find it. Ronald is the church's minister, and Chinaka's his first lady. Next, you will have the pleasure of meeting in the "Hitchhiker" the very arrogant Richard Rodriguez. He is the church's drummer, and Jessica, his wife, is the piano player. Next, you will be introduced in "My Past Doesn't Define Me," the overcomer, Armel Benjamin, is the church's assistant pastor. Lastly, in our final story, you will meet Blakeney Riddenburg, Ashlyn, and Ace McClain as they share their life stories in "The Chosen Ones." Each member's life story has been compiled in this book without farther delay. I present to you "Ordained Footsteps."

CHAPTER 1

"TAL'ITHA CU' MI"

Phoebe Westbrook was born in West Germany to Mr. and Mrs. Arnold Westbrook. Arnold Westbrook was a film producer who was nominated for and won several awards, including Oscar, Emmy Awards, and Golden Globe Awards for his movies. Phoebe's mother was an actor and a singer. She, too, had been nominated for and won several Golden Globe Awards and an American Music Award. Arnold had been in the field of entertainment for many years. Arnold worked on the same set as Harlow early on in their careers. Arnold and Harlow had mutual friends but never got the chance to meet one another. It wasn't until Arnold was asked to produce a movie starring Harlow and her leading man. Harlow was very fond of her leading man, but he paid her no attention because he knew her reputation.

Harlow was an industrious entrepreneur that danced in the hearts of many men. She broke more hearts than any heart surgeon could ever repair during their career. Arnold directed and produced many movies in which Harlow had the opportunity to play the leading lady. Arnold and Harlow, in many instances, came to one another's aid. Arnold and his wife Virginia and Harlow would become the very best of friends. Virginia and Arnold met as children. Arnold's father was married to Virginia's adopted mother. Arnold lived with his biological mother and visited his father on the holidays. During Arnold's visits with his father, he and Virginia were inseparable. Although Virginia was ten years older than Arnold, they had always had a close friendship. Upon their first meeting they instantly hit it off. He was always very protective of her.

He loved, respected, and adored her. He looked at her as the sister

he never had. After the passing of Arnold's father, Virginia began to

play a significant role in Arnold's life. Virginia took Arnold under her

wings, and in doing so, she fell in love with him. Arnold greatly

appreciated her. Although he loved her as a person, he wasn't in love

with her. Virginia was Arnold's only girlfriend. Virginia asked for

Arnold's hand in marriage. He feared losing her, so he accepted her

proposal. He felt as if he owed her. Virginia became the love of Arnold's

life. Arnold grew to love and adore her because she meant everything

to him. Virginia was unable to conceive. Although they had no children,

they secretly wanted children. Virginia, early on in their marriage, often

times got stressed about not being able to conceive. Virginia knew how

badly Arnold wanted children.

When stressed, Virginia often smoked excessively and drank alcohol to soothe her pain. Virginia was introduced to marijuana in high school. She soon replaced the cannabis with cigarettes. Smoking was a way of coping with stress in her daily life. Virginia would soon become a chain smoker and often smoked a pack of cigarettes a day. As the years passed, her past as a chain smoker would catch up with her. Virginia's daily routine would soon change as her health began to decline. She soon found herself constantly ill and occasionally had a loss of appetite which resulted in drastic weight loss. Virginia had unexplained pain that was often times accompanied by a shortness of breath. She was one who had never been big on doctors. She felt the doctor's job was to find something wrong with their patients. She had seen her share of hospitals growing up as a teenager.

Virginia's mother died of cancer when Virginia was a teenager. Before her mother's death, she had spent many sleepless nights beside her dying mother in the hospital's intensive care unit. Virginia had no option but to make an appointment to see her doctor. At Virginia's doctor's appointment, she would soon learn that she had lung cancer. Virginia and Arnold learned that Virginia has stage three lung cancer and is given three months to live. Arnold and Harlow are shattered when they learn of Virginia's cancer diagnosis. Harlow began helping Arnold with Virginia as her cancer rapidly progressed to stage four. On her deathbed, Virginia calls her family together to say her goodbyes. Virginia makes a special request to see Harlow and Arnold. Arnold tells Virginia that he vows never to marry again, giving his heart to another because his heart will always belong to her.

Virginia tells Arnold how much she loves him and wants him to be happy. Virginia tells him that the purpose of her calling an emergency meeting with the family to include Harlow. She wants to ensure that he will be taken care of upon her passing. She tells Arnold that she also cares for her dear friend Harlow and knows that she would make Arnold a great wife. She wants Arnold and Harlow to be happy and knows they will be happy together. She wants them to promise to take care of one another. Virginia feels what better way for them to be able to effectively care for one another than to get married. Virginia secretly knows that Arnold loves her but was never in love with her. She has witnessed on several occasions how Arnold looks at Harlow. Virginia knows that out of loyalty to her and their marriage, Arnold would never move on with his life without her approval.

She feels strongly that Harlow is Arnold's true soulmate. Upon

hearing the news, Arnold immediately cuts her off. Honey, I know you

are not feeling well, but what are you saying? Virginia intervenes,

assuring Arnold that she knows what she is saying. She asks Arnold

and Harlow promise that they will get married upon her death. Virginia

contends that she knows both Arnold and Harlow and that they possess

the characteristics that the other needs and desires. After Virginia's

passing, one year later, as promised, Arnold and Harlow got married.

Arnold asked for Harlow's hand in marriage, and she accepted. They

were married on a private island east of Kenya, The Seychelles. They

were surrounded by a host of their family and friends, many of which

were also celebrities. Arnold and Harlow came to know and love one

another.

Several years would pass before they knew Virginia was right in her choice. Arnold grew to love Harlow dearly, and they completed one another. He came to love Harlow as he had never loved any other woman. Arnold loved Virginia but loved Harlow in a much different capacity. He not only loved her, but he was in love with her. Perhaps, Virginia was correct in her judgment of character with the two of them. Harlow likewise loved and adored Arnold. They fit together like a hand in a glove. They complimented one another in every aspect. The couple grew to know one another very well. They often found themselves completing one another's sentences and usually knew what the other person was thinking before being communicated. Two years later, they would conceive and welcome their first child, Phoebe. Both Arnold and Harlow had remarkably busy careers.

The Westbrooks' lives not only revolved around their jobs, but their jobs were their lives. The cast and crew members not only worked for the Westbrooks but also spent quality time together off-set. They were the true definition of an extended family. After giving birth to Phoebe, Harlow continued to work. Upon Phoebe's birth, the cast and crews babysat her to help the Westbrooks. Phoebe was born with a silver spoon in her mouth. She was raised in show business. Phoebe's very first steps were taken on the stage of the set of one of her father's productions. Her very first words were those of a written script. Phoebe went to work with her parents and came home with them as well. The Westbrooks worked twenty-four hours a day, seven days a week. Phoebe, too, would soon begin acting.

Phoebe was given lines where she acted in commercials as she got older and began modeling and singing. Just like her mother, Phoebe had the vocals to surely move a crowd. Phoebe, just as her parents were born to be an entertainer. Phoebe was the spitting image of her mother. Phoebe not only sang like her mother, but she looked just like her as well. Phoebe had sandy red hair with enormous hazel eyes that often spoke for themselves. Phoebe's nannies, along with the staff and crew, took turns taking her and picking her up from school, acting auditions, and extracurricular activities at her private school. Phoebe was very popular in high school. However, Phoebe didn't let her career get in the way of her having a normal life like most teenagers. In her spare time, she enjoyed cheerleading and hanging out with her friends, just as most teenagers her age.

Phoebe dated many of the popular guys in her school. However, Phoebe never kept anyone around very long. Phoebe changed her boyfriends like she changed her perfumes. Many people admired Phoebe; she was an outstanding actress and singer. Phoebe had proven herself in many instances, and her reputation spoke for itself. Her career was very impressive. Although Phoebe was loved and adored by millions, her dad was the biggest fan of them all. Arnold and Phoebe had a very close bond because she was his miracle child. Phoebe was a blessing from God to Arnold. He had always wanted children and now finally had a beautiful "Baby-Girl," as he often referred to her. It wouldn't be long before the pass would repeat itself. On Arnold and Harlow's twentieth wedding anniversary, they decided to celebrate one another with a date night out on the town.

When Arnold doesn't come down to get in the car, Harlow decides to check on him. She finds him passed out on the bedroom floor; she notices that he doesn't appear to be responsive. Harlow calls emergency crews as they rush Arnold to the hospital. Arnold's x-rays revealed that he had suffered a mild stroke, but his problems were far from over. Arnold's blood work also revealed that he also had lung cancer. Arnold was baffled by the doctor's discovery. He could not understand how he could have lung cancer. He had never smoked a day in his life. Arnold and Harlow questioned the doctor's findings. They requested a second opinion which also confirmed the doctor's diagnosis. The physician explained to Arnold that although he wasn't a smoker, being around a heavy smoker and inhaling secondhand smoke was just as bad as smoking himself.

Arnold was reminded of the many years he was in the company of his late wife Virginia as she smoked a pack of cigarettes daily for years. Arnold's cancer had metastasized throughout his body, and he wasn't expected to live another month. Harlow and Phoebe felt as if their world had fallen apart. Arnold would die two weeks later, and Harlow felt lost without him. Phoebe decided to take a break from the limelight. She felt her acting was in vain since she lost her biggest fan. She struggled as she tried to cope with her father's passing. Phoebe's life began to spiral out of control. Phoebe started drinking excessively and experimenting with street drugs. Phoebe began to give up on life, questioning her purpose. Phoebe's self-esteem began to decline as her competition threatened her career. Phoebe was loved and adored by all except for the one that mattered the most, "herself."

Phoebe not only didn't love herself but pushed those that did love her away. It showed in Phoebe's actions that she wanted to be anyone except who God had allowed her to become. Phoebe had temper tantrums and threatened to harm herself when she didn't get what she wanted. However, it was all just an act as usual with her. Regardless of whether she was getting what she wanted, she still looked for a reason to end her life. Phoebe hated the person that she saw when she looked in the mirror. She had it all but still had nothing. Phoebe's peers would kill at the chance to be in her shoes or to live the lavish lifestyle that she led. She bought and owned her very own luxury home at the age of sixteen. Not only could she provide for herself, but most of her boyfriends were wealthy tycoons.

She was showered with lavish gifts such as the newest cars, yachts, trips, clothes, shoes, purses, and monetary gifts. None of those things mattered to her. Those things still were not enough for her. Despite how beautiful she was, she still was not happy with her appearance. Phoebe began to experiment with plastic surgery for the answer to her problems. She began getting cosmetic surgeries to enhance her beauty. Her first cosmetic surgery was a rhinoplasty. Months later, Phoebe decided to get lip fillers, a breast enhancement, and a Brazilian butt lift, and the list continued. Others looked highly upon Phoebe. However, she still wasn't happy with herself or how she looked. Phoebe got over twenty cosmetic surgeries before she began to be semi-happy with herself and the way she looked.

She still had an emptiness inside, as if something were missing, and was often depressed. She had accepted her father's passing and knew it was best for him that he didn't have to suffer. However, Phoebe tried to fill the void that she was forced to deal with daily. Phoebe continuously drank excessively and increased her drug usage to include hallucinogens. She liked the feeling she got when she was high. She felt as if the sky were the limit and that she could do anything. Phoebe, when high, most importantly, felt she didn't have to deal with the pressures of the world and the competition of having to stay on top. Her drug usage began to interfere with her work, making it difficult to focus effectively on her career. Many of Phoebe's friends were married with families, and all appeared to be happy in their lives. She wondered if having a family of her own would fill the void she constantly faced.

Phoebe decided to try her hand at marriage, hoping it would fill

the void she carried. She accepted a proposal to marry her best friend

and high school boyfriend, Axel. Phoebe and Axel were married in

Puglia, Italy. Phoebe and Axel months later gave birth to a handsome

baby boy that she named Phoenix. Although she loved her husband and

son, there was something still missing, her life was still incomplete.

Axel pleaded with her to see a marriage counselor to save their

marriage. Phoebe refused to seek counseling, filing for a divorce.

Phoebe did not love herself and felt incapable of loving Axel and their

son the way they needed to be loved. Phoebe and her husband divorced

after just two years of marriage. They shared joint custody of their son

Phoenix.

One night after wrapping up filming, Phoebe and her best friend of fifteen years decided to go out to celebrate the completion of Phoebe's new movie. Phoebe and her best friend Lauren decided to take Phoebe's new car. Phoebe's new car was a 2023 Bugatti La Voiture Noire specially designed by her. Phoebe and Lauren had their share of drinks. Soon after leaving the grand opening of Phoebe's new movie, they decided to go to the club upon consuming more alcoholic beverages. After leaving the club it was obvious that the girls were inebriated. Phoebe decided it would be best if she turned the driving over to Lauren. She had expressed interest to Phoebe in test-driving Phoebe's new car. Phoebe felt that now was the most opportune time. Lauren were an inexperienced driver she had only been driving for one year.

She was not used to the turbo power that Phoebe's new car possessed, along with her altered mental status. Phoebe climbs into the car's passenger seat, entrusting Lauren with her new car. Phoebe soon falls asleep. Phoebe dreams that she and Lauren is sitting in a beautiful green pasture. They appear to be having fun sitting telling jokes. Lauren as usual always told jokes that only she could comprehend and seemed extremely corny to Phoebe. After telling her joke Lauren without waiting for Phoebe's response would beat Phoebe laughing at her very own jokes. Phoebe, after hearing Lauren's laugh, which resembled that of a pig's squeal, she would also laugh. Phoebe's dream this time was different from all others. Phoebe's dream ended with Lauren telling her how much she loved her. Lauren tells Phoebe that she forgives her as she waves bye and vanishes.

Phoebe is suddenly in a tremendous amount of pain. Phoebe is woken by a cool breeze as she hears a soft chant, "Tal'itha cu' mi," as she is awakened by excruciating pain that radiates through her body as she is unable to move. Phoebe hears the voices of emergency crews. They explained to Phoebe that she was in a serious accident, but she would be okay. Phoebe looked around and noticed that she was entrapped in her new car. As she looks around for Lauren, she sees that Lauren is unresponsive and doesn't look well. The crews applied the jaws of life as they worked to free Lauren and Phoebe from the vehicle. Phoebe and Lauren are rushed to the hospital, only for Phoebe to find out days later that Lauren was pronounced dead on the scene of the incident. Phoebe, after learning of Lauren's death, is devastated. She blames herself for Lauren's sudden death.

She knows that if she had taken her shofar instead of allowing

Lauren to drive, knowing that she, too, had been drinking, she would

still be alive. An autopsy revealed that Lauren had been killed upon

impact from blunt force trauma sustained to her head. Phoebe also

suffered head and face trauma, and her x-rays revealed she had several

broken ribs, a broken back, and a collapsed lung. Upon arriving at the

hospital, Phoebe is immediately taken into surgery for what would be

her first of many surgeries. Days later, after Phoebe's surgery, she

immediately notices that she is unable to stand. Phoebe begins sobbing

because not only can she not stand, but she also cannot feel her legs.

Phoebe is unable to move her lower extremities. She begins to scream

and yell hysterically. Phoebe hired some of the best plastic surgeons,

orthopedic and neurologic surgeons, to perform her surgery.

As doctors prepare to perform a second surgery on her, there is very little that they can do. Phoebe already had a significant amount of scar tissue from her past cosmetic surgeries. They are unsure as to how successful the surgery will be. They are uncertain of how much more cutting on her body that her body can withstand. However, she is left with no option as they work to reconstruct her face and her spine. Phoebe undergoes many surgeries as they work to restore or come as close as possible back to her body's original appearance before her accident. Phoebe's doctor tell her that he have done all that he is medically able to do, and she has a forty percent chance of ever walking again. She sees herself in the mirror weeks after her second surgery. She immediately begins to scream as she throws the mirror to the floor, breaking it in disbelief.

Phoebe is visited by her mother, her ex-husband, and their son. She refused any other visitors stating that she didn't look acceptable. Phoebe immediately informs the staff that she desired not to have any other visitors. Phoebe tells Harlow about her dream about Lauren during the incident. Harlow tells her that it was Lauren's way of saying her last goodbyes to Phoebe. Harlow encourages her to be strong, ensuring she will be fine. Phoebe lies in her hospital bed, where she contemplates suicide because she had given up on life. Her life would never be the same. She feared that her family and friends would look at her differently. Phoebe feared that her career as an actress and singer had come to an abrupt end. Acting and singing were all she had ever done because it was all she knew. It was her foundation. Phoebe's career defined her as an individual.

Phoebe fell into a deep depression. She refused to allow anyone to see her, and she refused to eat, resulting in drastic weight loss. She felt as if no one understood what she was going through. She had finally realized that she had everything and still did not appreciate it until it was all being taken away. She took pain medicine even when she was not in pain. She felt if she were asleep, she would not be reminded of her incident and the fact that she could no longer walk. Phoebe many nights cried herself to sleep. One night after a long, intense day of physical therapy Phoebe felt hopeless. She concluded that she had endured enough and decided she wanted to end her life. Phoebe decided to ingest a hand full of opioids as she began to get drowsy. She hopelessly cried herself to sleep. As Phoebe falls into a deep sleep. Phoebe could never have imagined what would happen next.

She had always imagined herself going to heaven once her earthly journey was complete. She imagined being ushered into a beautiful mansion made of the finest gold, being reunited with her loved ones, and being at peace. Instead, Phoebe got the opposite. Creatures of all sorts visited her. She witnessed creatures that varied in height from two feet to six feet tall, many of which had multiple heads and tails, to include missing limbs. Phoebe grasped for her breath as she struggled to breathe due to the intensity of the heat. The heat was roughly 3000 °F, which was hotter than the sun's surface. The smell reaped in such a way that it was unimaginable. Phoebe knew that she had chosen hell as her home. Phoebe knew of God, although she didn't have a personal relationship with him. She had been to church a few times and had donated to the homeless.

She felt she had done enough to someday get into heaven. Phoebe felt that she never really had a reason to have a relationship with Christ. She had riches and fame, she had everything that she needed to survive. Sadly, her money could not buy her a place in heaven. Phoebe begins pleading with Christ to give her a second chance at life to make things right. She didn't want hell to be her home. She is quickly reminded that she was given multiple chances to come to Christ, and she refused each time. She is reminded how she had survived multiple plastic surgeries, two of which she was revived back to life. Her life was also spared in the car wreck that took her friend's life. Ungratefully, she has now tried to end her very own life. Phoebe pleads with Christ that if he gives her another chance, she will change her life and follow Christ, leading others to him.

Phoebe is immediately woken up following the dream by a soft voice as she hears the words "Tal'itha cu' mi" whispered, followed by a gentle breeze of air just as she had experienced following her accident. Phoebe was unsure of what it meant or where it had come from and why she kept hearing it. Phoebe looked up the meaning of the word "Tal'itha cu' mi" to see if such a word exist. She learned that the word was a biblical term found in the bible in, the book of (Mark 5:39-42). It was revealed to her that during her accident, she heard the lord's voice whisper to her, "Tal'itha cu'mi," which means "little girl" in Aramaic. It is given in reference to the biblical story in the gospel of Mark in which Jesus Christ resurrected a dead child with the words "Tal'itha cu'mi." It reads as following: And he came to the house of synagogue and see the tumult and them that wept and wailed greatly.

He said unto them why make ye this ado and weep? The damsel

is not dead, but asleep and they laughed him to scorn. When he put them

all out, he took the father and the mother of the damsel, and those that

were with him, and entered in where the damsel was lying. He took the

damsel by the hand and said unto her "Tal'itha cu'mi." It is interpreted,

Damsel, I say unto thee arise and straightway the damsel arouse, and

walked for she was of the age of twelve years old. They were astonished

with a great astonishment. Phoebe was taken to learn that she was so

special to our Lord and Savior that he refused to let her die during her

accident. She had to get up because there were works that she must do

in Christ Jesus. Her journey in life wasn't over, and he loved her so

much that he decided to give her a second chance to correct her life.

Phoebe immediately begins to feel remorseful.

How could she have been so selfish, thinking only of herself?

She was given another chance to make her life right in the eyes of her

lord and savior. Lauren, on the other hand, never got a second chance.

Phoebe began praying to God for forgiveness and thanking him for

loving her when she wasn't capable of loving herself. Phoebe was often

reminded of the story of "Tal'itha cu' mi" whenever she felt like giving

up. Five years would go by before Phoebe could stand up on her very

own. She was able to stand for short lengths of time before having to

sit down. Months later, while out at the park with one of her aids Phoebe

runs into an old high schoolmate. Phoebe and Quinn weren't friends but

knew of one another in passing. They had never had the chance to hang

out; they only knew of one another casually. Phoebe tried to hide her

face to avoid Quinn seeing her.

Quinn spoke to Phoebe as she continued on her way. Phoebe noticed that Quinn either was an outstanding actress or she didn't notice Phoebe's scars. Everyone else from Phoebe's past stares at her when they see her. Phoebe eagerly spoke back to her. Quinn was surprised by Phoebe's actions. In high school, Phoebe had always been in a rush, accompanied by her entourage, barely able to speak. Quinn began conversating with Phoebe. Quinn and Phoebe reminisced about high school. Before long they were catching up on the latest gossip. The girls enjoyed one another's company. They exchanged phone numbers and talked on the phone for hours. Quinn and Phoebe began talking on the phone daily. Before long, Quinn invited her to a show, but Phoebe was reluctant to go since she no longer looked the same. She wanted to stay out of the public eye because she was very insecure.

Phoebe also found it difficult to go to some of the places she once had since now she was wheelchair-bound and could only stand in short increments. Quinn informed Phoebe that it wasn't a show like she thought. In fact, it would be several appearances by different gospel artists. Many of them would preach and perform some songs from their CDs. It was a praise and worship festival. After fighting with Quinn for two days, Phoebe finally decided to attend the gospel festival with Quinn. Upon attending the praise festival and hearing one minister preach, Phoebe felt as if he was speaking to her precisely and to her life in general. Phoebe began attending church services regularly with Quinn. She enjoyed attending church services and looked forward to going. Phoebe was at peace in church. The feeling that she got was like never before.

Phoebe was now complete; the emptiness she had experienced for years no longer exist. She had finally found the answer to her problem. She questions whether it could be that God is the missing piece that she needs and desires. He provided the fullness that she craved. Having God in her life was better than any high she could have ever experienced with any alcohol or drug. She desired to know and learn more about God. She began to pray more, and she asked him to guide her. As things started to look up for her, she found herself no longer worried about the material things of the world. She was no longer concerned with how people looked at her. All she wanted was to live a life pleasing to God, always praising him. Nothing else mattered; she just wanted to be in God's presence.

Phoebe began to use her platform to speak to lost souls, men, women, and children, of all ethnicities. As she established a relationship with God, she grew to know and love him despite her situation. Phoebe knew that God was not only loyal, but he was a provider in a time of need and a healer in a time of sickness. She decided to try God, and she took him at his word. She asked and believed in God for healing and the strength to be able to walk again. Phoebe underwent physical therapy, and God healed her as she regained her strength in her lower extremities. She soon began walking without the help of a walker. As Phoebe started to grow spiritually, she began to care less about the things of the world. She began to seek Christ as she learned more about her earthly assignment. Phoebe was very grateful to God and wanted to find a way to help others just as God had helped her.

Phoebe opened her own acting theater, working with individuals of all ethnicities and status. She worked with low-income, the elderly, and those with disabilities. Phoebe told her story and how the Lord had spared her life everywhere she went because it was her testimony. It took Phoebe to almost lose her life to find out how blessed she really and truly was. Phoebe then decided that she wanted to work on putting her family back together. It all made sense to her God. God is love, and how can she effectively love without God? Now that she had God in her life and had him abundantly, she was capable of loving herself and others. Phoebe found herself going down the aisle for a second time with Axel in a private ceremony as Phoenix was their ring bearer. Phoebe and Axel vowed to love one another until death will they part.

Axel and Phoebe operate several organizations for underprivileged children and people in general. Phoebe has since given birth to a baby girl that she named Grace, for her name speaks for itself. God's Grace is sufficient. Phoebe and Axel work with many of the area's churches organizing donations. Phoebe likes to be able to lend a helping hand to those who are less fortunate. In our second short story, you will be introduced to the beautiful Mercy St. James is in "Lord, have Mercy."

CHAPTER 2

LORD, HAVE MERCY.

On the other side of town resides Mercy St. James, who thinks that the world revolves around her. Mercy thinks highly of herself and thinks she is God's gift to the world. Mercy and her friend Taytum are video models. However, Mercy is also a dancer and choreographer. She has choreographed many dance routines for several musicians. Mercy has also appeared in several videos and movies. Mercy and Taytum pride themselves on their appearance. It is important for them to look their very best at all times because they're both in the public eye ninety percent of the time. Both girls relied on cosmetic surgery to give them the look they desired. It wouldn't be long before Mercy would develop an addiction to cosmetic surgery. Mercy got routine cosmetic surgery of some sort yearly for the ten-year time span of her career.

Mercy had over thirty cosmetic surgeries performed on her body for various things. She struggled to maintain her image among the up-and-coming artist in the industry. She feared that her time was drawing near because the industry was beginning to change to accommodate the growing needs of society. She had always turned to cosmetic surgery as her scapegoat. Mercy being older, her body was changing, which required more complicated procedures. She had even acquired an infection numerous times from her surgeries but didn't let that stop her. Mercy's surgeries included a rhinoplasty, Brazilian butt lift breast implants, vein removal, and genioplasty/mentoplasty, to name a few. Mercy had features that consisted of a doll; she looked flawless. Not only was Mercy beautiful, but she had the kind of job that many people dreamed of, making a very impressive salary.

Mercy looked down on people who didn't look a certain way or make a certain income. She knew how beautiful she was. She felt as if everyone was beneath her, and no one was deserving of her. Many of her friends were celebrities. Mercy's boyfriend, Santiago "The Velvet Rose," was also a recording artist and was well-known and loved by millions. Santiago and Mercy were the model couple. Santiago and Mercy often toured together because she was also one of his backup dancers and his choreographer. Mercy's love for Santiago was undeniable; she adored him. She was very overprotective and often went out of her way to ensure others knew they were a couple. One day during dance rehearsals while choreographing a dance routine, she slipped on a wet spot on the floor, injuring her ankle.

X-rays revealed she had broken her ankle. Mercy was flown back to her home in Los Angeles following her injury. She would end up undergoing surgery and being out of work for months. Mercy was in severe pain and forced to go through therapy. Mercy feared that her injury would jeopardize her career. Santiago assured her he would be there for her every step of the way, both physically and financially, as she went through therapy. It marked the beginning of a troubled relationship between Mercy and Santiago. He was there for Mercy for the first two months as their relationship would soon become strained. As Santiago continues to tour, Mercy hears rumors of Santiago's infidelity. Santiago is photographed being intimate with other dancers as well as other musicians.

Santiago soon stopped returning her phone calls. Mercy began to struggle financially as her money became scarce, as she was now unemployed. She was forced to find other means to earn an income. Mercy is crushed and has no one to turn to for support. She runs into a mutual friend and fellow musician who invites her to a listening party. Mercy attends the listening party in hopes of running into Santiago at the party. She later learns that Santiago has extended his concert and is touring in China and will not be at the party. Mercy decides to attend the listening party alone. Mercy saw several of her friends in attendance at the party when she was introduced to a native of West Africa named Bongani Abara. Bongani was very diverse in the entertainment field. He worked both in front and behind the scenes. He was a videographer who also choreographed.

Bongani was a tycoon who had come to the United States to attend school. He was almost done with his studies in the United States and looking to obtain citizenship. Bongani was actively looking for a wife in the United States to assist him with becoming a citizen. He is immediately attracted to Mercy, but she pays him no attention because no man can compare to Santiago in her eyes. Mercy wanted nothing to do with him because he wasn't the type of man that she could imagine herself dating. Bongani was short and stocky in stature and wore multicolored clothing covered with patches that fitted him very baggy. His eyeglasses were as dense as an ice cube. Bongani's clothes complimented a style of his very own there were other West Africans present, but none dressed like Bongani. Although Bongani wasn't very appealing to many women, his personality made up for the fact that he wasn't very attractive.

Bongani was very sociable; he had never met a stranger he could befriend anyone. People of all status loved and respected him, and he had a smile that would melt your heart. He always looked for the good in everyone. Bongani was a fan of Mercy's work, and he admired her. He was excited to meet her. He tried to communicate with Mercy several times throughout the night, only to be belittled each time. Although he wasn't very fluent in English, it didn't take him very long to know that Mercy wasn't very fond of him. He soon came to realize that Mercy was out of his league. At the end of the party, Bongani waved to Mercy only to have her walk past him, never acknowledging him. The following day while speaking with one of her friends over the phone. Mercy's friend asked her why she was so hard on Bongani, stating that he was really and truly a wonderful person.

He began telling Mercy that Bongani was in the United States to attend college. He worries about returning home now that he is almost done with his studies. He tells Mercy that Bongani is actively looking for a wife to marry so that he can continue living in the United States until he gets his citizenship. As Mercy's friend talks about Bongani, she immediately cuts him off. She asks her friend why he cares about Bongani, stating that he is not the ideal man for many women in today's society. Mercy hears nothing else that he is saying upon hearing that Bongani is a tycoon, and he is looking for a wife. She feels that he is the answer to her financial problems. Mercy hates the idea of thinking about possibly being in a relationship, fake or real, with Bongani. She literally despised him and could not see herself being intimate with him in any way. Mercy laughs and tells her friend she must go.

She has more important things to be concerned about. Upon disconnecting the phone call, she gets a knock at the door, and as she opens the door, a piece of paper falls at her feet. Mercy immediately opens and begins reading the note when she notices it is an eviction notice. Mercy tried reaching out to Santiago but got no answer, as usual. After careful consideration, Mercy calls her friend back and gives him permission to arrange a meeting with Bongani and herself. The following day Bongani meets with Mercy to speak with her about his plan to become a citizen. Bongani explained to Mercy that he wasn't a citizen of the United States and he needed to get married to a US citizen so that he would be able to remain in the United States. He explained to her that he was a billionaire, and he would not only pay her a salary, but he would also pay all of her finances. She didn't have to work if she desired not to work.

Bongani wanted to be in a relationship with Mercy. She explained to him that for her to enter into their contractual agreement, he must agree to her dating other people. Mercy also told him that he too could date anyone he desired. Bongani, in desperate need of her help, decided to take her up on her deal. Mercy and Bongani got married and resided in separate homes, with Bongani agreeing to pay all of Mercy's living expenses. As time passed, Bongani tried on several occasions to establish a relationship with Mercy. He wanted to show her his appreciation. He tried several times to take her out on a date only to have her refuse each time. In many instances, he made her dinner only to have her complain about the dinner he'd prepared. Bongani wanted to know her likes and dislikes because he wanted to express his gratitude to her.

Mercy constantly reminded him that he wasn't her type and was only there due to an agreement. Despite how Mercy treated Bongani, he was always pleasant and considerate of her, being mindful that she was still his wife. Every chance Mercy got, she reminded him that he was beneath her, turning up her nose at him. Bongani was very attractive to her, but she always reminded him that he was only there for financial gain. In Mercy's eyes, Bongani was only a credit card with legs, nothing else about him mattered to her. Mercy was obsessed with herself. She was concerned that she looked flawless at all times. She was warned of the dangers associated with plastic surgery. Many surgeons refused to perform procedures on her, afraid of her chances of survival. It didn't stop her; she was determined that she would look her very best, even if it costed her life.

Mercy and Taytum were always in competition to see who looked the best. They constantly looked for the best plastic surgeons as they copied one another in procedures. Mercy's friend Taytum had plastic surgery to have her eyebrows lifted and to give herself a prominent jawbone. Mercy, like the outcome of Taytum's surgery. She decided that she too must have her jawbone reconstructed, and her eyebrows lifted. Taytum gave Mercy the contact information of a plastic surgeon located in Mexico. Mercy decided against her loved ones wishes to travel to Mexico for the surgery. Because Mercy refused to allow Bongani to travel with her. He hired an assistant to travel with her to provide assistance for her after the surgery. Her surgery went as planned. Mercy pulled through her surgery and returned to her home in Los Angeles without any complications.

She was instructed not to remove her bandages until the third day following her surgery. Mercy had several plastic surgeries in the past, but none was as painful as this particular surgery. On the third day following her surgery, Mercy awoke at the break of dawn as she was excited about removing her bandages. With her assistant's help, she began removing her bandages. As her assistant removed the last bandage, she noticed the sudden change of facial expression on her assistant's face as her assistant stared on in silence. Mercy asked her assistant what why are you looking at me like that? Her assistant was speechless, and as Mercy looked in the mirror, she didn't recognize herself. Her face was scarred and distorted, she had poorly connected skin with loose pockets. She looked to be roughly eighty years of age. Mercy began screaming and yelling, "How could you do this to me?"

She could not believe what she saw. She looked like a monster

of some sort. Mercy's assistant immediately runs to get Bongani. Mercy

tried to reach out to the doctor that performed the surgery, but he was

nowhere to be found. The office he used to perform the surgery days

earlier was now vacant. Mercy reached out to Taytum, who referred her

to the doctor. Only to be shocked by what she learned. Mercy arrived

at Taytum's home the following morning, where she immediately

spotted Santiago leaving. It was clear to her that he had stayed all night.

Mercy is saddened by what she sees. She refuses to allow him to see

her in this condition. She hides in the bushes beside his car. She wipes

the tears from her eyes. After Santiago leaves Mercy reemerged from

the bushes. Mercy bangs on the door Taytum just as she suspected,

comes to the door in her nightgown, where she immediately confronts

her.

Mercy begins yelling at Taytum," how could you do this to me?" How could you betray me? I thought that you were my friend. Taytum is stunned by what she sees. "Mercy, is that you?" She looks on in surprise, "what happened to you?" Mercy informs Taytum that the doctor she referred her to in Mexico, whom she was a patient of also, had botched her plastic surgery. Mercy is surprised by what she learns next. Taytum tells Mercy that she had never been a patient of the doctor herself and that she had looked him up on the internet. Mercy feared that her biggest fear had now come true. Mercy felt that Taytum not only betrayed her by stealing her boyfriend, but she also manipulated her. Mercy was disturbed by what she heard. Mercy was heartbroken by how she looked. She had no one else to turn to.

She feared what people would say when they saw her and how she would be talked about by everyone in the industry. Mercy unexpectedly turned to Bongani. They tried to find a surgeon willing to correct her botched surgery. She was turned away by many surgeons. They refused to take her on as a patient, seeing her as a liability. She had already had too many surgeries. Her skin had too many scars in some places and too thin in others. Mercy wore a veil covering most of her face to hide her botched surgery. Mercy looked unappealing. She went from having men eating out of her hands to not being able to turn heads at all. Mercy, in a last attempt of hope, because she feared being alone. She then began spending time with Bongani, and he made her forget about how she looked. He made her feel like the woman that she was. However, there was just one problem the time had finally come when Bongani was eligible for citizenship.

He was now a legal citizen, which meant that he no longer had to be married to Mercy. She never thought she would see the day when she asked Bongani not to leave her or their marriage. Mercy asked Bongani to consider staying in their marriage because she did not want to be alone and was concerned about ever finding anyone else.

He informed her that he must go because his time with her was up. Mercy cried profusely, she assumed that he didn't want to be with her because of the way she looked. Bongani told her that he didn't care how a person's outward appearance looked; he looked at their heart. The heart was a reflection of the inner beauty which was most important to Bongani. He explained to her why he could not stay with her. Bongani explained to her that he had come to know her since their marriage. He noticed that she was very mean and uncaring, and self-centered.

Even if she didn't get the botched surgery, he knew that he could never truly love a woman of her character. He tells her that she must change her ways if she is to ever get anyone to genuinely love and respect her. Letting her know that she must first love and respect not only herself but others as well. Lastly, he reminds her of the agreement that they had prior to entering their marriage. Reminding her that she incorporated that they were allowed to see other people. He had been dating his new love interest for one year now. They were madly in love and were looking to take things to the next level. He tells her that he has filed for a divorce. Bongani tells Mercy that he will continue to pay her rent for one year or until she can get on her feet. He tells her they will always be friends but could never be anything more. Bongani tells Mercy that if she should find a doctor willing to take her on as a patient, he would cover the expense.

As Bongani exits Mercy's home, she collapses to the floor in disbelief. Mercy feels as if a rug have been snatched out from under her as she feel like her life was in shambles. She feels as if everyone that she has ever loved, she has lost, including her very own self in a sense. Mercy questions God, she feels like she is being punished. Mercy prays, dear God, why have you allowed this to happen to me? What have I done so bad for this to happen to me? Not only have I lost my source of income. I have lost my husband and the only man that I have ever truly loved and not to mention even my self-respect. I cannot go out in public looking like this. God, if you give me another chance, I will do whatever it is that you want me to do. Heavenly father, I know that I haven't always been pleasing in your sight, but I will change. Lord, please allow me to find a surgeon willing to take me on as a patient and restore my face as close as possible to normal.

If you do this for me, I will afterward never in my life get another plastic surgery. Mercy refused to go out in public without her scarf. She found it difficult to obtain employment because most employers required her to remove her face mask. The only exception was if she could provide a medical prescription or proof of religious belief for her face covering. Mercy was a choreographer and hung around many celebrities, which made it hard for her to remain secluded. Mercy was not required to work when she was married to Bongani. However, since their contract had been fulfilled and he was no longer required to give her financial support, she needed to work. Mercy fell into a deep depression. She refused to come out of her home for fear of someone seeing her. She wanted to forget how she looked. She subsequently covered all of the mirrors throughout her home.

She battled with the demons of depression daily. As Mercy began to flip through the channels on her television. She comes across a gospel program on television. The minister spoke about how people will leave you, but God will never leave or forsake you. Upon hearing the topic, Mercy began watching the gospel program before being reminded of her botched surgery and finding herself angry with God. Mercy immediately turned the television off. Miraculously the television flickered and turned itself back on. She reached for the remote control to power the television back off again. The remote control fell on the floor where the batteries were ejected out of the remote control. Mercy retrieved two of the three triple-A batteries but could not locate the third one. The third battery wasn't anywhere to be found as she searched all over. Left with no option, she decided to watch the gospel program.

In the sermon, the preacher of the hour spoke about how many people worship other people and things overlooking God and not entrusting God. The preacher talked about how we must trust God and put him first in all things, and he will fulfill our needs and wants. As Mercy watches the sermon, she begins reflecting back on her life and the things that she had done, and what she could have done differently. Mercy thinks of the people that she had surrounded herself with in the past. Mercy thinks about Santiago and what her relationship was like with him. The minister is preaching from the book of Deuteronomy 5:7-9; I am the Lord thy God, which brought thee out of the land of Egypt, from the house of bondage. Thou shalt have none other gods before me. Thou shalt not make thee any graven image, or any likeness of anything that is in heaven above, or that is in the earth beneath, or that is in the waters beneath the earth.

Thou shalt not bow down thyself unto them, nor serve them; for

I, the Lord thy God, am a jealous God. (Romans 12:3-8) He also told

her by the grace given me, I say to every one of you; Do not think of

yourself more highly than you ought but rather think of yourself with

sober judgment, according to the faith God has distributed to each of

you. Mercy thought she was better than others, which is reflected in

how she treated Bongani. Mercy recalls how much she loved and put

Santiago first in everything she did, only to have him walk away from

her when she needed him the most. Not only did Mercy lose Santiago,

but she also lost her best friend, Taytum, and her husband, Bongani.

They all walked away from her when she needed them the most. Mercy

began praying to God for forgiveness and guidance.

Immediately following the completion of the gospel program, a commercial came on advertising a job opening for a choreographer with a local fine arts magnet school. It was a public school that offered classes to musically gifted children. Mercy thought that it would be the ideal job. It came with a sign-on bonus, it was a set schedule, and it was 5 minutes from her house. Mercy knew it was an act of God. She normally would not have been watching the channel her television was tuned to if it wasn't for her losing the remote-control battery. She would have missed not only the sermon but also the local advertisement for the job opening. At the end of the programming, Mercy spotted the third battery on the floor beside the leg of the chair. Mercy knew it would be the perfect job for her. She hated being out in public for extended lengths of time.

She was always concerned about who she might run into that would recognize her. However, she desperately needed the money and knew she would be the perfect candidate because her resume spoke for itself. Mercy submitted her resume for the position, and she immediately got a response the following day inviting her to come for an interview. Mercy was unsure how she would be received with her face scarf. Mercy arrived at the private school for her interview. When she was escorted into the interview room. The interviewer looked very familiar to Mercy, but she was unsure of where she had seen the interviewer prior to now. The interviewer promptly tells Mercy that she is free to remove her facial mask if she likes unless she is comfortable with it on. Mercy insists that she is comfortable and wants to keep it on. Mercy, unsure of what the interviewer will say, prepares to get ready to leave.

The interviewer begins asking her questions about her choreography. Mercy notices that the interviewer's voice sounds very familiar. As the interviewer proceeds with the interview at the end, she apologizes to Mercy for not introducing herself. And she introduces herself as none other than the one and only Phoebe Westbrook. Mercy is shocked to learn that it is the famous actress and songstress Phoebe Westbrook. Mercy was a fan of Phoebe's work. Mercy immediately apologizes as she explains to Phoebe that she didn't recognize her, stating to Phoebe that there were something different about her. Phoebe briefly drops her head as if she had heard it all before. She tells Mercy that there is no need to apologize as she begins to share her story with Mercy. As Phoebe shares her story with Mercy, Mercy is moved to tears.

In addition Mercy begins to share her story with Phoebe. She asks Mercy for permission to remove her face scarf to see the severity of her botched surgery. Mercy hesitantly removes her scarf. Phoebe goes over and hugs her and offers support. Mercy is surprised by what Phoebe says next. Phoebe wants Mercy to see her very own Plastic surgeon, and she also offers to pay for Mercy's surgery. Phoebe makes Mercy an appointment to see her very own plastic surgeon. Reluctantly, Phoebe's surgeon agrees to perform reconstructive surgery on Mercy. She underwent surgery twice before seeing a difference in her facial features. Mercy was able to stop wearing her face scarf, and her life was finally getting back to normal. But there was just one thing she had to go see Bongani to apologize for how she treated him throughout the years that she was married to him.

She had finally realized that she had a good thing, and she let him get away; it was not about how he looked. What mattered was how he treated her and cared for her when no one else was capable of caring for her. Mercy prayed, dear God, I thank you for touching Phoebe and her surgeon's heart to perform and restore my face too as close a normal as humanly possible. God, if you would just give me another chance to prove to Bongani that I am capable of being the wife he deserves. I had the man that I had always dreamed of and never even knew it until losing him. God, if you give me another chance to prove myself the next time, I will do it right. Mercy got dressed in her finest and decided to go see Bongani. She was determined that she was going to win his heart again. Mercy pulled into Bongani's driveway; she sat in her car for a few seconds to get herself together because she wanted to make the very best impression on him.

As she got up the nerve to get out of her car, she was now more confident than she had been in a long time since her surgery. Mercy rang the doorbell, and on the second ring, the door opened. There stood a lady with olive skin and long flowing hair who looked to be expecting a child. Mercy said I am sorry; I have the wrong house. I was looking for someone by the name of Bongani. The lady laughed no; you have the right house. I am Bongani's wife Dena. I can get him for you. Would you like to come in? Who can I tell him is here to see him? Mercy looks on in dismay as she is hurt yet again. No one, I am just an old friend who was just coming by to see him. Mercy turns and immediately walks back to her car and leaves. Several years would go by before Mercy gets another chance at love. Mercy and Phoebe were not only co-workers, but they had also become the very best of friends.

Phoebe invited Mercy to attend services at her church, and Mercy gladly accepted. After attending several services at Phoebe's church, Mercy decided to become a member. Phoebe introduced Mercy to Warren Pagan, one of Phoebe's friends. Warren was a respected gospel recording artist and civil rights activist who was also a member. Mercy and Warren hit it off instantly and before long was a couple. Mercy finally got a second chance at love, and she was sure to do it right this time. In the beginning, after learning what Warren did to earn a living, she was hesitant to date him. She was reminded of what it was like dating a musician when she dated Santiago. She didn't want to be hurt again. She felt that all musicians were the same. Warren pleaded with Mercy to give him a chance stating that he was different. He was a man after God's very own heart, which showed in his lifestyle.

From the first day Mercy went out with Warren, she was shown respect and treated like a lady. Mercy was thankful that she had given him a chance. Warren took Mercy on the road with him when he toured. The news of Mercy and Warren dating hit the blogs. Mercy and Warren were in love. Mercy was happy for the first time in her life. She was in a relationship that she not only loved but felt loved. Mercy and Warren's love for one another would soon be tested. A fling from the past would return to make trouble for Mercy and Warren. One day after a long exhausting day at work, Mercy would come home to a lovely arrangement of flowers sitting on her doorstep. Mercy opened the card as it read: Mercy, you are an extraordinary lady who deserves only the best from someone who really misses you. If you're not too busy, I would like to take you out for a night in the town. You are indeed the love of my life.

Please, be ready. I will be picking you up at 8:00 p.m. Mercy was excited, she knew how busy Warren had been in the studio recording, and she thought it was very thoughtful of him to take out some time to take her out for a date. Mercy was dressed in her finest as she waited for Warren to arrive to escort her on their date. At 7:59 p.m. Mercy's doorbell rang. Mercy opened the door, where she was greeted by a chauffeur driver and escorted to a Mercedes-Benz S600 Maybach. Inside the car, waiting was none other than her beloved Santiago. Mercy was stunned to learned that Santiago was her date. She was happy to see him but was angry with him and how their relationship had ended. Mercy immediately turned to go back into her house. Santiago jumped out of the car and ran over to her. He pleaded with her to go out on the date with him. He told her that he missed her and needed to talk with her.

Mercy promptly informed Santiago that she was no longer interested in him and now had a new love interest. Santiago pleaded with her to at least go out on the date just to hear him out. While out on the date, Santiago asked Mercy to give him a second chance stating that he had changed. Mercy, knowing his past, found it hard to believe him. Mercy went out with him to make amends with him. On their date, Mercy and Santiago had a wonderful time. They laughed and joked about past events and updated one another on current changes in the industry. They had such a lovely time, Mercy contemplated about seeing more of Santiago. The following day after sharing the details of her surprise date with Phoebe. She told Mercy that, according to mutual friends, Santiago was married ten months ago. Santiago was currently separated from his wife because of his infidelity.

Just as she had suspected, he had not changed. Mercy ceased all communication with Santiago, unwilling to be hurt again as she had been in the past. Mercy informed Warren of her and Santiago's date and begged him for forgiveness. Warren asked for Mercy's hand in marriage. They would date for five years before getting married. Mercy and Warren are both active members in their church. Warren sings in the church's choir. Mercy is in charge of the praise team where she choreograph dances. Mercy and Phoebe are youth mentors and often speak with the youth about the importance of self-love. Mercy shares her story with young women who just as herself fight with addiction to plastic surgery. She has helped hundreds of people, including celebrities, through her testimony. Santiago is now divorced, and on his second marriage, he still travels the country touring.

Bongani is happily married with three beautiful children. Taytum battles with drug addiction and is unable to maintain employment. In conclusion, there are many women in today's society who could relate to the women in the story in some way. Many women have a part of their bodies that they would like to change or has already altered in some way. (Leviticus 19:28) says, "You shall not make cuttings in your flesh for the dead, nor tattoo any marks on you, says the Lord our God. These prohibitions were done in honor of the dead, to propitiate their sins, or to gain God's attention. In our next short story, you will hear from the church's minister and his wife about the ironic events that brought them together in "God Decides."

CHAPTER 3.
GOD DECIDES

The Henson family were residents of Manhattan, New York. They were a great representation of an all-American family. Paul and Sarah Henson were the perfect couple with the kind of marriage that many couples work for years to achieve. Paul and Sarah Henson were highly respected and well-known in their town. They were loved and looked upon as model citizens in their city, and they participated in many of the town's organizations. Paul worked as a pediatrician, while Sarah worked for the local elementary school, where she would be nominated on numerous occasions as educator of the year. They were family oriented. They loved and cared dearly for people in general. The Henson Family spent a great deal of time networking and doing volunteer work in their city.

When the family were not volunteering, they made it a point to spend quality time together doing family activities. They were devoted in everything they set out to achieve. Chinaka Henson were Paul and Sarah's oldest child of four siblings. She adored her parents and vowed upon getting married that she would be an outstanding parent just as they were. Paul and Sara were incredibly supportive of their children. They attended all their children's school activities, such as parent teacher meetings, sporting events, and talent shows. The Henson family planned yearly lavish excursions for their children. They wanted to broaden their children's horizon. They wanted to introduce their children to the finer things in life. The Henson's had taken their family on all sorts of trips but had yet to have the opportunity to take a ski trip. They promised to take their family on a ski trip because they wanted to do something different from the past years.

The ski trip was promised three years prior. The Henson's had always instilled in their children that an individual's word was their bond. Although Paul felt uneasy about the trip, Sarah decided that the ski trip would take priority over everything else. Sarah was determined to oversee the promise that she and Paul made to their children. The Henson's decided to surprise their family with an all-inclusive trip to a ski resort located in France. Before boarding their flight, they faced several issues: missing their original flight to having their luggage stolen. Paul suggested to Sarah that they postpone the trip to a later date and take the children someplace else in the meantime. Sarah insisted on taking the kids skiing, reminding Paul of their promise. Against Paul's better judgment, the Henson's made the decision to go on with their trip as planned.

The family left for Meribel Ski Resort in Les Allues, France, for the ski trip and arrived at their destination, where they stayed for five nights and six days. The Henson's were having a wonderful time. They had a skiing instructor who worked with them individually. They were able to bond as a family while making friends with other families when tragedy struck. On the last day of the Henson's' ski trip, the family loaded their luggage in the shuttle to leave for the airport to return to their home in New York. Just as the family is about to exit the driveway of the resort, Chinaka thinks that she has left her cell phone behind. Chinaka asked her father to request that the driver returns to the lodge as she noticed her cell phone was missing. After returning to the resort and exiting the car, Chinaka immediately spots her cell phone jammed in the car's seat.

Upon Paul Henson exiting the vehicle, he sees what he believes to be a child trapped in the snowy slopes. Paul's love for children would not allow him to walk away from any child without providing some assistance. Paul Henson had dedicated half of his life to providing medical care to children. He was also one of the most loved pediatric doctors in his area. Paul immediately jumped into action, putting on his skiing gear and going down the slopes against his wife's wishes. Paul was thrown off course, losing control which caused him to slam into a tree, knocking him unconscious. Paul was rushed to a nearby hospital. He would be put on life support for three days. He was pronounced brain dead two days before his 50th birthday. It was later discovered that the child trapped in the snowy slopes was actually a doll left behind by a child.

How could the family trip that started out with overwhelming fun and excitement have gone so wrong? The Henson family returned to their home in New York City to pick up the pieces. Chinaka blamed herself for her father's untimely death. Chinaka felt that the incident would have never occurred if she had only looked harder for her phone and never asked the shuttle driver to return to the resort. Chinaka's mother found it extremely difficult to cope with losing her one and only love and trying to adjust to her life without him. Paul was Sara's soulmate. They had known one another since grade school. They had begun dating in high school and decided to get married after graduating from college. The family prepared to say their farewell to Paul. Sara was devastated by his death. She was surprised when she learned that Paul did not have an insurance policy or a will.

Paul had his own office and was an independent contractor. Sara's life insurance policy with her employer was just enough to cover the cost of Paul's funeral expenses, leaving no extras for bills. The money they saved was enough to pay the bills for several months. Eventually, Sarah was forced to get a second job to afford to keep the family home and maintain the family's finances. Sarah struggled to support not only herself but also her family. Eventually, the family home would be foreclosed on. Sara was forced to move into a less expensive home in a more affordable area of town. Sarah Henson was in a place different from the one that she had always known. Sarah, confused, angry, and afraid, sat day and night depressed. as she wondered how the only man that she's ever loved and that had ever loved her could no longer be in her life.

Sarah would soon begin drinking alcohol uncontrollably and abusing prescription painkillers as a source of comfort. Sara desired to have the same level of comfort that she got physically and mentally when she began ingesting the opioids. When she did not get the same comfort mentally, she began using more harsh drugs. Sarah's dependence on prescription drugs led to recreational drug usage, which eventually led to her downward spiral. Daily tasks that were once very simple became extremely difficult for Sarah to complete. She would soon be asked to resign from her job as an instructor. Sarah went from being nominated as teacher of the year to now being band from the school's premises. Sarah was told that she could never teach again in New York City for her refusal to get help for her drug dependency and her participation in the illegal sale and distribution of drugs to minors on school property.

Sara began to lose everything in two years' time that she and Paul

had spent half their lives building. Sarah was unable to keep a roof over

her and her children's heads. Sarah eventually would be evicted from

her apartment. Sarah traveled from one homeless shelter to another with

her children. Hiding from her family and friends out of embarrassment,

refusing to seek help out of pride and fear of what others may think of

her. School officials learned of Sarah's homelessness upon

investigating what appeared to be bite marks on her youngest child.

Upon conclusion of the investigation, it was discovered that the bite

marks were those consisted of a rodent. The child was promptly treated

and placed into Child Protective Services. The courts ordered that

Chinaka, and her younger siblings be placed in foster care temporarily

to allow Sarah the time that she needed to get herself together.

A few days later, Chinaka awoke one morning to learn that her other siblings had been taken by her uncle Edward, her father's oldest brother, all with the exception of herself. When Chinaka contacted her uncle, he told her that she was the blame for his brother's untimely death. He told her if she had never asked to return to the retreat, his brother would still be alive, and things would have been different. Chinaka's uncle told her she was not his biological niece and needed to contact her family. Chinaka's uncle informed her that the Henson's had adopted her when she was ten months old. Chinaka was told that she was a native of Monrovia, located in West Africa, and her birth name was Chinaka Babette. Chinaka sat dazed and confused, unsure why she was being told she wasn't a part of the only family she had ever known; surely the Henson's were her parents?

Chinaka sat sobbing and trying to make sense of everything. Chinaka wondered if it was the reason why she did not look like either of her parents. Chinaka had a darker skin tone, and she stood out from the rest of her siblings. She wondered what was her uncle's motive for providing her with the information. Chinaka turned to her mother, Sarah, for moral support and to get answers. Chinaka escapes from the orphanage to look for her mother, Sarah, as she searches for answers. Chinaka locates Sarah in an abandoned home known as the areas slum area on the south side of the city. She confronted Sarah with the information that was given to her by her uncle. Sarah burst into tears immediately. Sarah explained to Chinaka that she was raped as a young child and wondered if she could have children. Sarah and Paul decided to adopt Chinaka after several failed attempts of their trying to conceive.

She explained to Chinaka that she and Paul had tried numerous times but could never seem to conceive. It wasn't until after the help of fertility treatments they were able to have children. Sarah tells Chinaka that if she could do it all over again, knowing what she knows now, she would still have adopted Chinaka as her daughter. Chinaka, mourning her father's death and now learning that her parents are not really her parents, begins to question God. Chinaka, currently homeless, goes back to her Uncle Edward and begs him to take her in. Edward refuses to take Chinaka in, blaming her for his brother's death. Edward tells Chinaka that the only thing that he will agree to is buying her a one-way ticket to return to her biological family back in Africa. Chinaka refused to return to a life with which she was so unfamiliar. Edward requested Chinaka leave his home immediately and only return or have contact with her siblings once she decided to take him up on his offer.

Chinaka, with no place to go, returns to the abandoned home in search of Sarah. Chinaka and Sarah try to cope with the daily challenges of staying alive. Chinaka is overcome by the daily stress of the world picks up her mother's bad habits. She would eventually turn to alcohol and prescription medication as a source of comfort. Chinaka and her mother traveled from one abandoned home to another, seeking shelter. Chinaka was discovered by a government official behind an abandoned building going thru the garbage in search of food. She was placed back in Child Protective Services. She traveled in and out of several foster homes. Chinaka, tired and uncertain of her future, decided that she had no other alternative but to reach back out to her uncle Edward. Chinaka hoped that her uncle had changed his mind. She desperately needed a place to live or, worst-case scenario, to take him up on his deal.

As previously agreed, Edward's feelings still had not changed. He bought Chinaka a one-way ticket to Africa to reunite her with her biological parents and family. Upon arriving in Africa, Edward arranged to have someone meet Chinaka and escort her to her family. She was taken to a very poor village where little English was spoken. She was met and embraced by her biological parents, who introduced her to others in her family. Chinaka was very grateful for the opportunity to meet her parents and the rest of her family. Chinaka was shown survival skills for daily living. Chinaka tried to adjust to life as it was in Africa. It was very different from where she had come from and the life that she had grown accustomed to in New York City. Chinaka disliked her village and found it extremely difficult to adjust to life in Africa.

She was frequently picked on by the people of the village. They felt as if she had lived a very sheltered life and had no survival skills. Chinaka stood out from others in her family and the village. She could not speak their language and had no knowledge about the African peoples' customs or traditions. A year would pass before she would reach out to her uncle Edward via mail, pleading with him to help her to come back to the United States. Her pleas went unanswered. Although Chinaka was raised in the Baptist church, she did not have a personal relationship with God for herself. She heard others saying what he had done for them. Chinaka had never prayed to God for herself. She had always relied on her parents to pray to him on her behalf. Chinaka had no idea what to say, but she knew she needed some help and needed it immediately.

This time she did not have her parents to call upon for assistance. She had to call upon the name of God for herself. She only knew the daily bread prayer she recited every night before bed. After reciting the daily bread prayer, unsure what to say next, she began talking to God.

God, I don't know any fancy prayers, nor do I have a fancy vocabulary. God, I really need you right now. I heard that you are a God who can do all things. In fact, I was told that you are a miracle worker. If that is who you are, that is if you are a God at all. I need your help. I am in an unfamiliar place, and I do not know anyone I can trust or where I can turn. If you are who everyone says you are, would you please help me to get back to the United States? I have no money, no transportation, and no one I can call upon to help me other than yourself.

If you would allow me to return to my family in the United States. It is at that time that I will truly believe in your existence and know that you are a miracle worker. Upon completion of Chinaka's prayer, she was called upon to retrieve some water from a local stream to help wash members of her family's clothes. One month later on the way home from school. Chinaka was cornered by two teenage guys who insisted on Chinaka following them into an abandoned home. When she refused, one of the teens pulled out a blade and threatened to stab her if she did not go with them. Prior to reaching the porch of the abandoned home, a stray dog ran across one of the guy's feet out into the road in the path of an oncoming car. The driver of the vehicle swerved to avoid hitting the stray dog running off the dirt road into a nearby wooded area.

The driver immediately stopped the car and jumped out, marching over to the teenagers to voice his concerns about them not watching their dog more closely. The driver noticed Chinaka visibly shaken and crying profusely. Both teenagers immediately ran away, leaving her behind. Chinaka stood as she cried uncontrollably; the driver was unable to stop her from sobbing. Chinaka finally stops sobbing as she notices one very important detail about the driver. She notices that she can understand him very clearly. She notices that he is speaking English and is an American. She explains to the man what had taken place before the stray dog ran out in front of his car. The gentleman empathized with her telling her that he was sorry to hear that such an awful thing had happened to her. Letting her know that he was glad that he was able to help her.

The gentleman told Chinaka that he was not from Africa. Explaining to her that he was just there on an assignment. He told her how hard of a time he has had trying to comprehend the African native language. He asked her if she would be interested in assisting him, agreeing to pay her in return for her services. Chinaka told him that she was not very proficient in the African's native language, and, in fact, she was just learning their language. The gentleman introduced himself as Ronald and refused to take no for an answer from Chinaka. Ronald worked for The Department of Social Services. In his job role, he worked with people from all walks of life. Working with Ronald, Chinaka could make enough money to afford to buy herself the daily necessities she needed to live comfortably. Ronald's assignment in Africa had come to an end taking him back to the United States.

Ronald requested to meet with Chinaka in person at his office because he had some pressing issues that he wanted to discuss with her. During their meeting, he tells her that his assignment in Africa had come to an end. He would be going back to his home in the United States, which happened to be in New York City. Ronald told Chinaka that he would love for her to come with him. He has enjoyed working with her and would like her to continue to be his assistant, but he knew how much she would miss her family. Chinaka assured Ronald that she would be perfectly fine without her family. She, without hesitation, agreed to travel back to the United States with Ronald. She was overcome by emotions. Ronald found himself consoling her again just as he had consoled her upon their first meeting, but this time it was tears of joy.

After arriving in the United States, she now knew without a shadow of a doubt that there really and truly was a God. He may not have come when she wanted him, but he was on time. Chinaka began to search for her mother and her siblings. It now had been two years and six months since she had last seen them. Things were still as they were when Chinaka left two years earlier. Chinaka continued working with Ronald as his job routed him back to Africa several months later. Chinaka respected Ronald but refused to return to Africa a second time, stating that she had had enough to last her a lifetime. Ronald returned to Africa a second time, leaving Chinaka in the United States. Chinaka ran across an old family friend Mrs. Pickens. Mrs. Pickens was an elderly lady from the neighborhood where Chinaka lived before her father's death. Mrs. Pickens never had children of her very own.

However, she always had a soft spot in her heart for children.

Mrs. Pickens provided many of the neighborhood kids with cakes and

pies that she would make from stretch, never asking for anything in

return. Mrs. Pickens and Chinaka became the best of friends picking up

where they had left off years earlier. Mrs. Pickens was concerned for

Chinaka and cared for her dearly. Mrs. Pickens and Chinaka both

agreed to have Mrs. Pickens adopt Chinaka as her foster parent. As

things are coming together for Chinaka, another tragedy will soon

strike. Mrs. Pickens enrolled Chinaka in classes to get her General

Educational Development (GED). As Chinaka's life is getting back on

track, she suffers another setback when she tragically loses her new

foster parent. Chinaka is typically greeted by Mrs. Pickens at the front

door taking her book bag and escorting her into the kitchen for a

scrumptious home-cooked meal prepared just for her.

One Friday, after coming home from school, Chinaka enters the house and immediately smells something burning. She immediately enters the kitchen, where she notices a pot on the stove; it appears the water has boiled out of the pot, causing it to burn. She knows this is unlike Mrs. Pickens, and as she looks over, she spots Mrs. Pickens lying on the floor beside the table. She immediately dials 911, where they dispatch an ambulance. A neighbor follows the ambulance to the hospital with Chinaka. As she arrives at the hospital, she is devastated when she learns that Mrs. Pickens has died. An autopsy later revealed that Mrs. Pickens had died from a heart attack earlier that morning after Chinaka had left to go to school. Chinaka is forced to drop out of school to get a job to care for herself. Chinaka is introduced to "the wonderful world of adult entertainment," as she sarcastically summarizes it.

There were some benefits that came along with the business, both positively and negatively, primarily negative. Chinaka, by the age of twenty, owned two luxury homes, one of which was a five-bedroom, three-bathroom mini-mansion, and five luxury cars. In the beginning, Chinaka enjoyed her job and considered herself the luckiest woman alive. She had a fun job making the kind of money that most people her age could only dream of. Chinaka started out as a stripper and worked her way up to the title of adult entertainer of the decade; most of her customers were celebrities. Chinaka would eventually start her very own adult entertainment club that was operated twenty-four hours, seven days a week. Chinaka got the chance to appear in several music videos. Chinaka was at the top of her game until it would all be taken away from her in a slit second.

Chinaka was cited by the Internal Revenue Service (IRS) for not paying her property taxes. Chinaka's business, her house, and her cars were all taken by the Internal Revenue Service (IRS), which led to her downfall. Chinaka lost everything she had worked hard to establish. She struggled to get back on her feet. She returned to the strip club because it was all she had ever known. The competition was now much greater because she had gotten older and faced some health problems. In many instances, she was forced to interact with the customers on a different level, eventually leading to prostitution, drug abuse, mental and physical abuse. Chinaka became disinterested in "the wonderful world of adult entertainment." Chinaka wanted to quit the adult entertainment business. It started out as a fun and easy way to meet people, entrepreneurs, and celebrities while making some quick cash.

Chinaka only had a seventh-grade education and had no trade other than the adult entertainment business. Due to her limited education it was difficult for her to find a job. Working in the adult industry she was used to making a six-figure salary. Chinaka had been raped on several occasions and even, in one instance, beaten, robbed, and left for dead. Chinaka resorted back to her old habits. She began drinking heavily and using recreational drugs, which resulted in her using them daily. Chinaka could see herself turning into her mother. Chinaka, just as her mother had in the past, began using drugs as a means of escaping her problems. Chinaka refused to allow drugs to rule her life just as it had her mother. Chinaka made the decision to get out of the adult entertainment business. But was she too late?

As a result of her constant battle with drugs and alcohol abuse, along with her unskilled trade, her health began to fail. Chinaka was diagnosed at the age of thirty with a rare form of bone cancer. After being diagnosed with cancer. It became increasingly hard for her to maintain employment. She was no longer able to perform. Chinaka fell on hard times and was forced to file for bankruptcy. Chinaka had always had a plan in life and had not always made the best decisions; not knowing which way to turn decided that this was the end for her. While trying to cope with losing her possessions and living on the streets of Brooklyn. Chinaka found herself in and out of jail. One morning while in the county jail, Chinaka woke to a fellow inmate standing over her, informing her that if she had been a second later waking up that she would not have woken up.

The individual referred to herself as Nato for her temperamental ways. Nato tells Chinaka she must consider herself very lucky. The day of their meeting was Nato's first official day of "being back" to what is considered to be mentally stable. Chinaka unwilling to let Nato know of her fear of Nato. Chinaka sarcastically informed Nato that she was still vacationing and unsure of her return. Chinaka soon learned that she had been placed in the jail's psychiatric ward. Chinaka and Nato became the best of friends during the remainder of Chinaka's jail stay. Upon being released from jail, Chinaka returned to her old ways. Chinaka was often depressed and contemplated suicide. After several failed attempts to end her life one year later upon, Chinaka getting out of jail. Chinaka was found in an abandoned home where she would lay in a pool of blood with a small bullet hole just beneath her chin.

It was later learned that the abandoned house was where Chinaka, as a teen lived with Mrs. Pickens briefly before Mrs. Picken's death. Chinaka again survived what turned out to be her third suicide attempt. Chinaka woke up weeks later happy that she had another chance at life but yet sad that she still had to work through her daily life's challenges. Chinaka, at the age of thirty-four as she, lay in her hospital room, where she goes regularly for treatment due to complications sustained from her self-inflicted gunshot wound and the constant abuse of her body. Chinaka had always heard others say that prayer changes things. She knew from the one time she prayed to return to the United States how her prayer was answered. One-night Chinaka decided to take a back road thru a dark alley as she talked to herself aloud, "God, I am so tired of living like this.

My life is anything except enjoyable, and I don't know why I am still here. Unexpectedly, a male wearing a black ski mask jumps out, demanding she give him all her money. Chinaka tells the masked man that she doesn't have any money. He insists that she is lying, pulling out a knife and stabbing her before running off. Chinaka quickly loses blood and becomes weak as pain radiates through her body. She is unable to cry for help as she falls to the ground. Chinaka had contemplated suicide many times before, but she had never experienced anything quite like this very experience. As Chinaka's lifeless body lies on the ground, she sees herself like never before. Chinaka sees herself as if she were looking at herself on a 3D movie projection screen. Her body lays on the ground motionless, limped over her purse. Chinaka asks, Lord, is this really happening?

Am I dead, or am I in a horrible dream? As the ambulance and police crews arrived on the scene and began working on her. She overhears one of the ambulance crew members saying I think she's gone. As the crews work to revive Chinaka's lifeless body. Chinaka began to pray as if she had never prayed before. Chinaka recalled her mother telling her to always have faith in God for what she was praying, and it shall be granted. Chinaka began to pray from her heart. When she sees herself on a large projector screen speaking in front of a group of children, telling them not to be consumed by life's troubles, she suddenly sees another projector screen where she sees herself standing on stage in front of a large audience. On the second screen, she is giving a speech about her life story, and a lady looking like her mother, Sarah Henson, sits looking on as a member of the audience.

As she began to pray, she prayed, "Lord, I know that I have not always done what you have asked of me. I know that the life I have led hasn't been pleasing to you. I have tried to end my life numerous times, and all have failed. Lord, it seems like everything that I have decided upon and have tried none of them seems to work." Chinaka hears a soft voice saying: Until you seek me doing my will, what you do will not work for you. My will is not your will; nevertheless, my will is going to be done. I have given you several chances to recognize me, and I have proved to you that I am the "GREAT I AM" numerous times, and you still fail to acknowledge me. It was I that sent the dog spelled "GOD" backwards to save your life, and you still tried to end your life, and yet you are still ungrateful. After hearing the voice of God and knowing that her works had not been pleasing to him.

Chinaka cries as she prays, "Dear Lord, please do not let me go

this way. I know you have given me several chances, and I was still too

stubborn and set in my ways to praise and recognize you. God if you

give me another chance, I will forever praise your name. I will never

attempt another suicide for as long as I shall live. God, I did not know

that the future in which you hold in your hands for me was so bright

and promising. All I have ever only experienced to this point was hard

times and a life full of broken promises which brought heartaches and

pains. Please, God if you would just give me another chance at this

thing called life to prove to you that I can be all that you would have

me to be and more." As Chinaka prays she sees the third screen where

the ambulance crews continue to work on her lifeless body.

Chinaka starts to cry profusely when she hears one of the ambulance crew members says, "I have a pulse let us get her to the hospital." Chinaka wakes up a few days later in the intensive care unit. She is greeted by her nurse who promptly apologizes for disturbing her rest. Chinaka tells the nurse that seeing her is the best present that she could have ever asked for. Chinaka begins to pray Lord thank you for hearing and honoring my prayers and giving me a second chance at life. Chinaka lay praying as she is overcome by an abundance of tears followed by a feeling of calmness. The feeling that she got was like nothing that she had ever experienced, it was one that was indescribable one that could not be explained by any scholar. The feeling that she got was as if someone or something had taken over her body but there was no one there at least that she could see. No drug or alcohol of any type could ever compare to the feeling that she got.

It was a very different feeling, one that was very pleasing, one that was memorable, a feeling that reassured her that everything was going to be alright. Chinaka suddenly notices a beautiful book that immediately grabs her attention out of the corner of her eye. As she glanced off to the table beside her bed, she saw what appeared to be a very unique book. The book contained a ray of beautiful colors: orange, purple, lime, yellow, and pink. As she opened the book and began reading it, it contained a list of African and Nigerian names. Chinaka looked to see if her name was in the book since her uncle informed her that she was a native of Monrovia, located in West Africa. Chinaka had never known the meaning of her name until this point. Chinaka was surprised by what she would come to learn. Chinaka's name was not only in the book, but it was also a Nigeria name which meant Chinaka (God decides) Babette (Promise of God).

For most of Chinaka's life following her adopted father's death, she had always tried to decide on what she perceived to be correct and just for her life. The answer as to who decides on the journey of Chinaka's life was revealed in her very own name. Chinaka Babette's Nigerian name means God decides and the promise of God. After learning the true meaning of her name, Chinaka vowed to live her life by the true meaning of her name and to forever seek God in everything that she does. Upon learning the true meaning of her name and waking up to a second chance at life after a near-death experience at the hands of someone other than herself, Chinaka's life would forever be changed. The perpetrator of Chinaka's assault and attempted murder was later captured. It wasn't the perpetrator's first time being in trouble with the law.

He had committed similar crimes against other young women. He was charged with attempted robbery, attempted murder, and unlawful possession of a weapon during the commission a crime. He was sentenced to fifteen years in prison. Sarah Henson finally comes to grips with Paul's death. Sarah decided to donate some of Paul's belongings to the local charity. She wanted to move on with her life while keeping the family tradition alive. Sarah runs across a vanilla envelope with some paperwork that belonged to Paul. She had never seen the envelope prior to now. Opening the vanilla envelope, she notices what appears to be Paul's final will and testament with a letter. The letter reads as follows. To Sarah, my beloved wife, I apologize for leaving you so soon. We had always fantasized about growing old together.

My journey here on Earth is complete. We all have a set time here on Earth before departing to our permanent home. I know that we will someday be reunited again. I pray that you will find it in your heart to forgive me. I had contemplated putting off our ski trip. I knew it would mark the end of my journey with you and our beloved family. However, we have always taught our children that our word is our bond. I would rather go knowing that in my passing. I had the chance to see the smiles of joy and happiness on our kids' faces rather than leave them with unfulfilled promises and without having the opportunity to truly say "goodbye." Please, let Chinaka know that she is and will always be my lovely daughter in my heart. Sarah reads Paul's will and discovers that Paul has left her and each sibling an abundance of stocks and bonds, and property, along with a lockbox of cash.

The assets that Paul left his family was worth billions of dollars. Paul did what he did best, even from the grave provided for his family in their time of need. After reading Paul's letter, Chinaka was able to stop blaming herself for her father's untimely death and move on with her life. Sarah initially questioned why she and her family had to go through the trials and tribulations that they endured. She no longer questions she knows it was God's will. The trails and tribulations that they faced made them grateful, humble, and most importantly brought many of them to Christ.

Chinaka decided to try her luck once more. She went back to school, where she received her high school General Educational Development (GED).

After receiving her General Education Development (GED) certificate, she enrolled into a local university in New York City. While attending class at the university, Chinaka ran into her old employer and friend Ronald, whom she credits with saving her life. Ronald was pursuing a master's in theology. Ronald and Chinaka began studying together, and their friendship blossomed into a beautiful love affair. Chinaka received a master's degree in behavioral psychology. She graduated with the highest-grade point average in her graduating class. After graduating from college, Ronald and Chinaka got married. Chinaka decided upon leaving her native homeland of West Africa to stay in contact with her West African family. Many years had passed before she learned of her West African family's existence, and now time was of the essence.

She knew she could never call Africa her home because she was a New Yorker at heart, but she could not run from the truth that it was her roots. She felt to deny her African roots was to deny her very own existence, and she could no longer live a life of lies. Chinaka had now rededicated her life back to Christ, and he is not only love but also the truth. To get to know her family and build a bond with them, she and her husband arranged for several members of her family to come to the United States. She made it a point every summer and major holidays, such as Thanksgiving and Christmas, to spend quality time with both her American and African families. They took turns traveling to the United States, or she would travel to Africa. Her family enjoyed visiting the United States. They felt that the United States was not only beautiful, but the opportunities were endless.

While other members of her family felt that Americans were spoiled, sheltered, and materialistic. The African traditions were much different when compared to the practices of the American people. American styles were much different than what they were accustomed to. Initially, it was quite an adjustment for both Chinaka and her family. Sara, her adopted mother, also opened her home to Chinaka's West African family. She welcomed them with open arms. Chinaka and Sara would soon learn how different things were among the families. Their lifestyles were very unrelatable. She had to not only show them the way of life as it was in the United States, but she also had to adapt to their way of life. Chinaka hired a translator to teach her family English and herself their native language. Chinaka would go on to work for child protective services, where she worked with children in foster care.

Chinaka wanted to make a difference in the lives of foster children that were a lot like herself. Chinaka's husband was sworn in as a preacher, and he would eventually start his very own church. Chinaka also worked with many of the area's local schools whenever her schedule permitted. Chinaka would become an inspirational speaker traveling the world and speaking to billions of people, sharing her story, and inspiring many others. Chinaka has been able to share her life story and inspire people from all walks of life. Chinaka no longer receives chemotherapy for cancer. She has been in remission for fifteen years and no longer must be seen regularly for her self-inflicted gunshot wound. Sarah Henson is ten years sober and an active member along with Chinaka's siblings in the church that Chinaka's husband oversees.

Chinaka's uncle Edward begged her for forgiveness for his role in contributing to her life's trials. Chinaka forgave her uncle because she knew that it was God's will for her to find out her true identity, which allowed her to meet her biological family and her husband. Although Chinaka forgave her uncle, Edward, she wondered if he truly ever forgave himself. Edward began drinking alcohol heavily. One morning when Edward did not show up for work, the police were called to do a wellness check. They would find him sitting in his recliner with several empty beer cans and half a gallon of whisky on the table in front of him. An autopsy later revealed he had died from a massive heart attack hours earlier. The family was devastated when they learned of his death. Chinaka gave Edward a lovely homegoing celebration.

Chinaka through her travel ministry, has had the opportunity to meet several other members of her West African family. Chinaka's goal is to save as many souls as humanly possible before leaving her temporary Earthly home. I pray this story will be used to uplift and encourage the many Chinaka's of this world. In our next short story, you will hear the life story of the immensely arrogant Richard Rodriguez, our church's drummer, in "The Hitch-Hiker."

CHAPTER 4

THE HITCH HIKER

Richard Rodriguez was a small guy in stature with an enormous personality. He was raised in the small town of Blairsville, Georgia, with a population of 720. Richard was the second oldest of four siblings. Mr. and Mrs. Rodriguez made every effort to raise their children in church. They would attend church services on Sundays and bible studies throughout the week whenever their schedules permitted. Richard's parents were authoritarian parents when it came to their children. Richard's parents had a strong presence in their children's lives. Richard's parents believed in disciplining their children when they were wrong and rewarding them when they were right. Growing up as a child, Richard was often reprimanded for his behavior.

Richard was stubborn as he refused to listen to anyone, including his very own parents. He did what he wanted when he wanted, regardless of the consequences of his actions. Growing up, Richard's sisters and brother feared their father out of respect and did as they were told. On the other hand, Richard was always the risk taker and wanted to see how far he could push his father. Richard lived in the moment. He was the opposite of the rest of his siblings and demonstrated the total opposite of how they were raised. The rest of his family members were very humble and obedient. Richard was any and everything except humble or obedient. Richard was very loud and obnoxious, a thrill seeker, and was often the source of confusion. Richard felt as if he were the black sheep of the family. Richard felt the pressure of having to prove himself.

Instead of doing what was right and just to prove himself, he did the opposite. He had *no* limitations; he participated in everything and anything that he felt would validate him as the ultimate bad boy. Richard's parents found themselves constantly having to clean up his mess resulting in them being disappointed in his choices in life. Richard would bribe his sisters and brother to help him do things he knew were wrong. When his sisters and brother no longer wanted to participate, he would threaten to tell their parents. Richard as a teenager, led a life of crime; he conned, robbed, and sold drugs; there wasn't anything about him that represented good intentions. He always managed to find a way to hurt everyone that ever loved him. When it came down to making a dollar, he cared about no one other than himself. He would hurt anyone that got in his way.

His main objective was to acquire earthly riches, and he stopped

at nothing to achieve his goal. If it weren't for him being the spitting

image of his father in his father's younger years, they would question if

he belonged to them. Richard and his father looked like twins. Mr. and

Mrs. Rodriguez could not understand why he was very different from

the rest of their children. The Rodriguez family was well-known in their

town because of Richard. In high school, he was the running back on

his high school football team and a track star. He dated most of the

popular girls in high school. He was also famous for his constant run-

ins with the law. His confrontational ways kept him in trouble. He was

a magnet for trouble. Wherever he went, trouble seemed to follow. He

felt as if he was above the law. Some may even say that he danced to

the beat of his own drum.

Richard liked to prove himself as worthy of being called the town's thug. He had beaten up several guys from the neighboring town no one wanted to get on his bad side. He made fun and games out of terrorizing those that wasn't a part of his crew. He thought that it made him look tough. Richard thrived off the fact that he was well-known and a menace to society in every aspect. Richard was also known for his wild nature. He believed in having fun at all costs. It showed with the type of people that he kept in his company. The Rodriguez kids were all, except for Richard, well-behaved children and made above-average grades. The Rodriguez kids all, except Richard, knew what they wanted to do in life at an early age. After graduating from high school, they went off to college. The time had come for Richard to go off to college.

Although Richard went off to college, he had no idea what he wanted to do in life. Mr. and Mrs. Rodriguez hoped that while in college that he would learn some valuable life skills. Many of Richard's high school classmates attended the same college as him. While in college, Richard maintained his bad-boy image. In college, he became more popular than ever. He earned a scholarship to attend one of the best schools in Georgia. Richard's scholarship was granted on the basis he maintained a 4.0-grade point average and he continued to play football. Richard and his roommate Bradley had a party every other night. Richard and Bradley were known to have some of the most unpredictably wild parties. People looked forward to attending their parties. Everyone that was anyone could be expected to be seen at their parties.

Richard and Bradley constant partying and drinking got out of hand. Richard's grades began to fall, and his scholarship was in danger of being taken away. Early one Sunday morning, after partying all night, Richard awakes to find Bradley unresponsive. Richard finds Bradley lying on the bathroom floor face down, unresponsive as he panics and calls for help. Emergency crews rushed Bradley to the local hospital as doctors fought to save his life. They learned that he had ingested a variety of drugs to include fentanyl and crystal meth. Bradley's stomach is pumped, and he is given a dose of Narcan.

Naloxone, also known as Narcan, is a drug used to treat drug overdose in an emergency situation. Richard had no idea that Bradley was experimenting with drugs of any sort. A short time later, Bradley is revived and survives.

Bradley's parents immediately withdrew him from the college, insisting he move back home to attend school. While In college, the harsh reality hit Richard. Richard soon learned that he had to grow up and become the man his parents reared him to be. He could no longer rely on his parents to rescue him whenever he got into trouble. Richard would learn that the competition was steep. He was now just a number, and there were other football players that were just as good as he was, if not better. Richard had to work harder to prove himself. He had to find a way to stand out from the rest. Richard was the last to be recruited for a professional team. He was drafted and began playing professional football. Richard would play for a year before being forced to leave the game. It would not be long before he would suffer a severe injury to his knee and be forced to sit on the sidelines.

Richard had to undergo surgery for an anterior cruciate ligament

(ACL) injury, followed by a meniscus injury. Richard's football career

was over before it got started. He was forced to retire from the game of

football. Just as things were beginning to come together for him, it all

ended abruptly. While his other sibling were settling into their

professional careers, he was settling back into the house with his

parents. Richard's oldest brother worked as an engineer for (NASA)

National Aeronautics and Space Administration. Richard's sisters also

had professional careers. His older sister worked as a charge nurse in

the medical intensive care unit for one of the largest hospitals in Los

Angeles, California. His youngest sister worked as an attorney in

Atlanta, Georgia. Most of the Rodriguez's children went off to college

and finished and obtained rewarding careers, except for Richard.

He could not deal with the pressure of not being on top and out in front of the crowd, it began to get him down. Richard didn't know how to adjust to life as it was off the football field. He was too ashamed to face his other siblings and felt like a failure. Richard returned to his old habits, but this time it wasn't for financial gain. Richard himself became his very own biggest customer in drug distribution and usage. Richard began abusing his prescription medication and drinking excessively to cope with his daily stresses. He soon began buying other people's prescription medicine which proved to not be strong enough for him. He was later introduced to other drugs. However, cocaine was his drug of choice. He began battling with the demons of depression and addiction.

In his mind, he didn't feel as if he had a problem because he felt

he could stop by himself at any point in time. He replayed the pictures

in his mind of Bradley's lifeless body laying slumped over on the

bathroom floor and how Bradley had almost died from an overdose of

a mixture of drugs. He knew he had to stop but didn't know if he had

the willpower. It was the only thing that soothed his pain. He battled

daily with the constant pain from his knee injury and the mental anguish

of being unable to play the sport again. Richard felt as if he had to have

others around him to validate him. The people that hung around him, in

the beginning, were with him for their very own personal gain; now, he

had nothing to give, not even himself. He knew that throwing parties

would be an effective way to get the company that attracted the

attention that he desired.

This time without Bradley's help, Richard began throwing parties night and day where he hosted his own parties. Richard's parties always managed to get out of hand, and in many instances, the police were called out to intervene. Richard began to sink into a deep depression. He stopped taking care of himself. He would go days without showering or eating, and he began isolating himself from his friends and family. He had given up on life. He had contemplated committing suicide several times. Richard had gambled away most of his money and used the remainder to support his addiction. Richard lost his home and was forced to move back home with his parents. A month later, after moving back in with his parents, he decided to treat himself to a night out on the town at the local bar and grill.

Richard was excited to see his old high schoolmates and learn how they were doing after high school. Richard's ex-girlfriend, who he still cared for deeply, congratulated him on making the team to play professional football. Richard thanks her for her warm wishes and informs her that he is currently out due to an injury. She sat with him at the table, giving him her undivided attention until she learned that he had a strong possibility of never playing professional football again. She immediately excused herself and went to the restroom, only to never return. Richard later spotted her at the bar. He noticed that she was flirting and conversating with another athlete, who was also recently signed to play in the (NFL) National Football League, before exchanging phone numbers. Richard watched them leave the bar together as she purposely avoided making eye contact with Richard.

He was very hurt by his ex-girlfriend's reaction. He felt as if a ton of bricks had fallen on him. Richard quickly popped pills into his mouth as he chased them down with alcohol. After having numerous shots of whiskey, drunken Richard staggered as he made his way to the bar's door. Robbie refused to allow Richard to drink and drive. Richard's friend Robbie tried unsuccessfully to convince him not to drink and drive. Richard refused to listen to Robbie. Richard insisted that he wasn't drunk and decided against his friend's better judgment to drive himself home. Richard waited until Robbie turned his back and stole his keys off the bar. Richard immediately staggered out of the bar and got into his car. When Robbie notices what Richard has done, he runs out of the bar only to see Richard's car circling around the parking lot.

Robbie attempts to stop Richard before almost being struck by the vehicle. Finally, Richard pulls out of the bar's driveway hitting and running over the curb at high speed. Bystanders outside the bar and grill immediately knew that Richard's driving wasn't a good idea and that he was in trouble. Richard can be seen as he visibly struggles to hold the car on the road while driving under the influence of alcohol and illegal drugs. Richard can be seen driving down the center of the road as he approaches and runs thru the stop sign at a four-way interception. The car speeded thru the interception as it disappeared into the night. Richard realized he was more intoxicated than he thought. Richard was the risk taker that he was naturally. He was determined not to let the alcohol get the best of him, as he is very stubborn. Richard was determined that he was going to drive himself home.

Further on down the road, Richard manages to avoid oncoming cars as he drives on the wrong side of the road. Just as Richard is about to cross the bridge leading into his county, he spots a hitchhiker. The man stood alongside the bridge waving a handkerchief as motorist passed. Richard stopped to give the hitchhiker a ride, as he barely missed hitting the man with his car. Richard stopped, and the hitchhiker got into the car. Richard asked the hitchhiker where he was on his way. The hitchhiker told him that he was on his way to his mother's house, which happened to be a few blocks away. As Richard drove down the street, the stranger did not seem to be phased by Richard's driving. The man never even bothered to put on his seatbelt. Richard hit several signs while the hitchhiker was in the car. When Richard looked at the hitchhiker, he noticed that the man never even flinched.

Richard asked the man if he, too, had just come from the local bar and grill. The man told Richard that he had come from his father's house and decided to step out to run some errands. The man sat quietly before telling Richard he was on the wrong path. Richard was very familiar with his hometown and knew it like the back of his hand. He could drive the area with his eyes closed because it was the only place he had ever lived. Richard repeated the wrong path. Richard responded to the stranger by apologizing and introducing himself to the man in the same way in which he did everyone. Richard was very arrogant, and it showed in his mannerisms.' Richard told the stranger I am sorry that I didn't introduce myself. I figured you would know me just like everyone else. However, I am none other than the one and only Richard Rodriguez professional quarterback for Georgia.

If, upon getting to know you if I like you, I will request your name if you are worthy to keep around. Now as you were saying something about my being on the wrong path. The stranger responded yes; you are on the wrong path. Richard sarcastically told the man I see that I must educate you. I have you to know that there are only two roads that lead in and out of the town of Blairsville. Since you're so smart, I want you to tell me which should I be driving since I am on the wrong path? The hitchhiker informed Richard that the path that he was referring to was not the path to his mother's house. The hitchhiker told Richard that he would surely get to where he needed to go. However, his goal on this day was to provide Richard with assistance to get to the place he desired to call home.

The stranger says to Richard you seem to be very intelligent, so why is it that you do the things in which you do? Richard stares out the window, not responding to the stranger's comment. The man asks Richard, unlike me, will you, sir, get to where you desire to call home, traveling down the path you're traveling? Richard, still slightly under the influence of drugs and alcohol, not understanding what the gentleman was referring to, looked at him. Richard answered yes, this road leads to my home. Why do you keep asking me if I am on the right path and if I know where I am going? Richard laughs," I have had a few beers, but *hell*, I imagine it will get me at least near my house." The stranger looks at Richard with a straight face and says. "I find it rather ironic that you would use that word as your choice of wording."

Richard looked at him in confusion and asked him what word are you referring to? The stranger tells him the word *"hell."* The stranger informed him that the road that he was taking led to one home and one home only. The stranger advises Richard to reevaluate his life before it's too late. He warned Richard that *"hell"* would surely be his home if he didn't reevaluate his life. The stranger told Richard that he was traveling down the wrong road in life and that he needed to get on the right road if he was to make it to his predestined home. Richard was now sobering up and baffled by what he heard. Richard asked the man how is it that one avoid taking the wrong road. The man explained to Richard that if he were to avoid taking the wrong road, he must be made aware of some of life's most important rules.

There were several things that he needed to do, and the first one was to repent and turn from his wicked ways. Richard got a weird feeling that the stranger was no ordinary man. The stranger was different from anyone he had ever encountered. Richard was not afraid, but he felt as if, after the encounter, that his life would never be the same. It did not make sense, but it felt right. It usually took him a few hours to sober up from the cocktail of alcohol and hallucinogens. This time it took him less than half the time than normal. Richard tried to make sense out of it. All this time, Richard thought the stranger was only talking about his physical travels. However, the man meant both his physical and spiritual journeys in life. Richard now realized what the hitchhiker meant.

Meanwhile, the stranger informed Richard that the road he was travelling on would surely end, but not in the way he would like it to. As Richard spoke to the gentleman, the man appeared to have known more about Richard than he was aware. Although Richard knew many of the townspeople, he had never encountered the stranger. Richard had lived in Blairsville, Georgia, most of his life. He had seen all parts of Blairsville, Georgia, but as he continued to travel the road, it all began to look unfamiliar. The hitchhiker wanted Richard to see what his future holds if he chose the wrong road. The man referred to the wrong road as the road of damnation. The man informed Richard that if he wanted to know what the future holds for him to continue to watch the videos of his life. He wanted Richard to see what would happen if he stayed on the wrong path.

In the first scenario, the man showed Richard a glimpse of his childhood and what it was like for him as a toddler. The stranger shared with Richard things about himself and members of his family that no one else knew. Richard noticed that various stages of his life up to adulthood were shown on an enormous projection screen as they traveled. The hitchhiker showed Richard, his former roommate Bradley's lifeless body lying on the bathroom floor of their dormitory room. The hitchhiker told Richard that God wanted to open Bradley's eyes so he would know that his life could all be ended in a matter of seconds. The hitchhiker told Richard that God allowed him to see Bradley in that condition so that he would know that the same could happen to him. However, he may not be as fortunate to survive as Bradley.

The hitchhiker tells Richard that the incident was a warning from God to Richard, and the warning comes before destruction. The stranger shared with Richard what would have happened had he continued playing professional football. He tells Richard he would have become famous like he had always dreamed; however, not in the capacity Richard had expected. He would have become an overnight success for being the first athlete to have the largest rise and fall from grace in the history of the sport. His fall would be much more talked about than his accomplishments. His fall would leave him with health issues that would forever haunt him. Richard would not be able to deal with the pressures of the world. Richard's health problems would lead him to experiment with prescription drugs, leading to recreational drug usage and heavy drinking.

Richard's excessive drug usage and alcoholism will cause him to take the life of a longtime friend in an unforeseen car accident. As Richard observed the videos of his life, he noticed that many events had already taken place and saw why the man was warning him that he was going down the wrong path. Richard knew that he must turn his life around immediately and get on the right path. Richard intern decides to take his own life because he cannot deal with the guilt of taking his friend's life. Richard's mother cannot deal with his death. His mother mourns herself to her very own death. Richard's mother's death has a profound impact on his family. The family is never the same as they then becomes divided. Richard noticed in the video that as time passed, everyone he loved and cared for was no longer around.

He found himself losing them all, and the most astonishing part of the video was that he was asked to observe his background scenery very closely. In the beginning, Richard noticed several beautiful flowers, trees, and green grass. As the video played, he began to notice the beautiful flowers that contained an array of colors began to wilt and die, and the grass and trees that were beautiful and green had also withered and appeared to be dead and brown in color. The ground began to dry out and crumble. The stranger told Richard that's what the road to damnation looks like, so choose ye wisely this day. Richard looked over to the man and asked him what happened. The stranger said well, you gained the world and lost your soul. You made *hell* your home. In the second scenario, the man shared with Richard what his life would be like if he chose the right road.

The man told Richard that if he chose the right road, which he referred to as the road of eternal life. The man told Richard that things may start out tough, but things will become easier as he remains on the road of righteousness. The man warned Richard that he would lose some things, too, include the friendship of people along the way. He told Richard not to be discouraged because he would not need the things and people he lost. The things that he loses, he will get them back in double portions double for his trouble. Those things are being removed to make room for the new people and things he will receive. Those things and people will be replaced with better quality than he lost. The stranger told Richard that he would not want for anything and that everything he encounters will be blessed. He will be blessed coming and going; every piece of land he steps upon will be blessed.

Everything that he touches will be blessed beyond measure. The man told Richard that he would be blessed with a beautiful family. He showed Richard a glimpse of his future wife and children. He informed Richard that the love and acceptance that he sort after he would find in his family. He revealed that the unconditional love that Richard would have for his wife and children would be given in return to him. The man tells Richard that he will lead others to Christ by sharing stories of his life's trials and tribulations. The man tells Richard that he will be the glue to hold his family together. He will encourage other family and friends to change their lifestyles. The man tells Richard that the things he has seen are just the beginning of the rewards he will reap if he chooses to take the right road. The stranger informed Richard that he could not begin to imagine the things that would be given to him.

Richard would have favor that would be bestowed upon his life

for his works and obedience. If it were still Richard's desire to be

famous, he could be famous for God, and in this, he will be a bigger

success than he could ever imagine. At this time, they had arrived at a

fork in the road that Richard had never noticed until now. Richard asked

the man which direction he should travel. He told Richard that the fork

and the preceding roads represent his life. It was a road map of his life.

The stranger told Richard that although he could not tell Richard which

road to take in life. He told Richard that if he repented of his sins,

believed that Jesus died on the cross for the sins of this world, and asked

God to come into his life and direct his footsteps, he would be fine.

(Acts 3:19; Prov 28:13) The stranger tells Richard that it's not an easy

walk, but it is one that is most rewarding.

And that he must decide which road he wanted to travel in life.

He told Richard that when choosing one's direction, it should be

selected with careful consideration. The man tells Richard it is now in

his hands as to which road he will decide to take. The man tells Richard

that they have arrived at his stop, and he must leave. Richard looked

over but only saw a light pole in a wooded area. Richard turned, looking

to the man to confirm that they were in the right place. I thought you

said you were going to your mother's house. The man points near the

wooded area alongside the road. Richard turned to reevaluate the area

when he noticed three older homes sitting in a row side by side. The

area where the homes stood looked outdated, and the location was

poorly lit. Richard was barely able to see them. Richard knew that it

would be hard for the stranger to see how to get to his mother's house.

There appeared to be no lights on in the inside of either one of the homes. Richard showed the man how to use his flashlight. Richard welcomed him to take the flashlight with him for assistance with getting into the man's mother's house. The man exits the vehicle, Richard watches him walk in between two of the three homes. Oddly, Richard notices that he never sees a light of any kind come on. Richard repositions his car to see in between the two homes as he turns on the car's bright lights for better visibility. Richard is stunned when he doesn't see the stranger. The man was nowhere to be found. Richard wondered if he had gone into either of the homes. He questioned how the stranger could have gained access to either of the homes in less than a second. Richard was left baffled. He was concerned about the safety of the man that he now referred to as friend.

The gentleman had helped Richard, and now he wanted to return the favor. Richard proceeded on with his trip. Although the stranger's reference was geared more toward Richard's life. Richard had now come to a fork in the road while traveling in his car that he had never noticed until now. Richard wondered if this could be a test to see how much attention he had paid to the stranger's directions. Perhaps a test to prepare him for what was to come in his personal life. Richard was unsure of which direction he should take. He used the information that he was provided by his friend. He prayed and recited the words that his friend had shared with him. He noticed that one road was straight and extremely narrow while the other road was wide. Richard, like many people, was afraid of heights and afraid of the unknown.

He also noticed that the road that appeared to be narrow looked from an angle to be going upward. In contrast, the road that was the widest appeared to be going downward. Both roads were paved in a foreign material that was unfamiliar to him, with beautiful green grass along the side. Richard opted to take the widest road, but something deep within told him to take the narrow straight road or else he would be forever regretful. Richard decided to take the straight and narrow road. Three days later, Richard woke up in the local hospital. Richard was greeted by several of his family members and friends. Richard was told that on the night of his driving under the influence (DUI), upon going around a curve, he was unable to keep the car on the road running down an embankment. There were no other cars involved. Richard's car was the only vehicle involved, and he was, in fact, fortunate to be alive.

Richard did not recall the incident nor the moments leading up to the incident. However, he does remember the hitchhiker that he picked up and dropped off the night of his incident. Richard inquired about the stranger, whom he now credited with saving his life, whom he had picked up the night of his accident. Richard's parents tell him that there were no accounts, according to the police, of anyone else ever being in the car with him before the accident. Richard's loved ones feel his story is not trustworthy. They knew his memory was altered the night of the incident due to the alcohol and hallucinogens he had taken. Richard told his friend Robbie about the stranger he had given a ride to the night of the incident and how he had helped him. Richard explained to Robbie that he had picked up the stranger along the highway before crossing the main bridge that led into town.

Richard explained that the man stood waving a handkerchief as motorist passed in an attempt to hitchhike a ride. Richard's friend immediately cuts him off, describing the man that stood waving the handkerchief and the clothing that he wore. Richard's friend told him that the gentleman he speaks of had been killed along that same bridge twenty years earlier while trying to get a ride to his mother's house. The man's mother stayed a few blocks down the road from the bridge. Richard's friend tells him that there have been reports of motorists witnessing the man's ghost standing along the bridge, waving a handkerchief occasionally. Richard was stunned by what he heard. Richard knew that he was under the influence of alcohol and hallucinogens, but he knew that the gentleman that he saw was very real.

In fact, the man had told him his life as it was as a child and what it would be like if he did not change the road that he was on. Richard thinks back; it all began to make sense as to why the guy knew so much about him and why he did not need a flashlight to see how to get into his mother's house. Richard listened to Robbie and thought about the events that had occurred the night of his accident. Robbie quickly motioned to Richard to turn up the volume on the television. There were new details in the hit-and-run that occurred on the night of Richard's incident along Interstate 2. The incident happened near the bar and grill where Richard visited the night of his accident. As Richard and Robbie watched the news broadcast, the newscaster announced that the victim of the hit-and-run was out of critical condition and expected to make a full recovery.

An arrest in the hit and run was expected to be made on today, announces the newscaster. Robbie looks at Richard as they both agree that the streets will be much safer after knowing an arrest will be made. Shortly afterward, they receive a knock on the door. Two police officers were escorted into Richard's room by the hospital's security. One of the officers asked Richard how he was feeling. Richard tells the officer that he has been feeling fine until now. The officer asks Richard for information identifying himself. After verifying Richard's identification, they read him his rights. The officers told him that after a thorough investigation, all evidence led back to him as the driver of the vehicle that was involved in a hit and run. The officer identified the vehicle involved in the hit and run as a 2020 jeep wrangler black in color. The front bumper was found at the scene.

Richard also drove a 2020 jeep wrangler that was black in color.

He felt that he was in a horrible dream that was never-ending. He was

taken from his hospital room to the county jail. Richard remained in jail

for a week before a bond was set. After he was released on bond. Robbie

comes to visit Richard at his home. Richard explained to Robbie that

he hit a few traffic signs and bumps in the road but did not recall hitting

anyone. Robbie explained to Richard that although he did not remember

the incident, it still occurred. Robbie asked him how he could be sure

that he did not hit anyone. Richard explained to Robbie that he had

picked up the hitchhiker shortly after leaving the bar and grill, and they

had been together most of the night before his accident. Richard insists

that the hitchhiker can confirm his story. Robbie told Richard it would

be a good idea if the hitchhiker he had given a ride wasn't a ghost.

Robbie warned Richard that if he thought that he was in trouble before trying to explain that he gave a ride to a ghost. Robbie laughed; not only will people not believe you, but you will be committed to the jail's psychiatric ward. Richard was unsure of what he could do, if anything, to fix the situation. Richard remembered the word of advice that the stranger had given him if he was ever in trouble and needed some direction. He remembered that the first thing was to repent, and the second was to pray, but there was just one problem the stranger meant in terms of direction. Richard wondered if these very same rules would apply and be effective for him in this situation. He began to repent, but there was just one thing he could not remember the prayer that the stranger recited to him. He was forced to pray on his own what was in his heart.

He wasn't sure if it would be as effective as the stranger's prayer or if it would even sound as good as the prayer that the stranger recited to him. Uncertain of what to say, Richard began to say what was in his heart and mind. After Richard finished praying, a feeling of easiness came over him that he had never experienced. Richard wasn't sure of how things would turn out. However, he felt deep down inside that everything would be fine. In Richard's prayer to God, he asked to be brought thru his ordeal stating that he would change his life for the better. Richard would soon start rehab to gain full use of his legs back. His right leg suffered the most damage in the car accident. While going thru physical therapy, Richard began to reevaluate his life. He regretted many of the decisions that he had made in life. Richard desired to learn more about Christ.

Richard reads his bible daily. Richard's loved ones began to see a change in him. He was invited to attend services at his mother's church. Richard attending services at his mother's church brought them closer than they had ever been. He looked forward to attending church services every Sunday. He refused to allow a Sunday to go by without being there. He learned to accept responsibility for his actions. He decided to seek treatment for his drug and alcohol abuse. In physical therapy, he began to make friends with other patients. He developed a very special friendship with a lady named Jessica. Jessica, just as Richard was in an accident and going thru physical therapy to learn how to walk again. Richard and Jessica were motivated and helped one another to get thru physical therapy. They had a unique relationship.

They motivated and brought out the best in one another. Richard and Jessica began seeing one another apart from treatment. They enjoyed being in each other's company. Richard and Jessica began dating. Richard knew that Jessica was the one that he wanted to spend the rest of his life with. Richard and Jessica became members of his mother's church, where they joined the choir and usher boards. Richard was most happy when he was with Jessica. He had not been happy in years. Richard's life was finally beginning to look up. Just as Richard is finally making progress in life, his past would come back to haunt him. Three years later, Richard received a letter in the mail that his court case involving the hit and run had finally come up on the court's calendar. The courts were very behind; there were far too many cases than they could accommodate.

Richard knew that he had to tell Jessica about the incident. The court date was quickly approaching. It was a possibility that he could be getting some jail time and possibly never see her again. However, he wasn't sure how she would react to his news. He wondered if it would change how she felt about him or if she would still want to be in his life. Upon Richard and Jessica's meeting, Richard told Jessica that he had something that he needed to speak with her about. Jessica told Richard that she also had some news to share with him. Jessica told Richard that she was finally going to be able to get justice for her incident. Jessica told Richard that she had been given a court date so that she may finally get justice for her crime. Richard tells Jessica that he is happy to hear her news and that he is in her corner.

Richard informed Jessica that he also had gotten paperwork to attend court for his incident. Jessica and Richard had never discussed the details surrounding their incidents. He could not recall the details surrounding his incident, and it was too hard for Jessica to talk about her incident. When inquiring about the date and time of the court proceedings, they were both surprised to know that they had to appear on the same date and time. She had never known her perpetrator's name as she read her paperwork; she was surprised by what she learned. Richard, the man that she had grown to love and trust, was the accused perpetrator of her crime. He was being charged in her hit-and-run. Jessica could not believe what she was reading. Jessica looked at Richard in disbelief. It was you; it was you all the time.

Richard looked at his court paperwork and noticed that Jessica's paperwork was identical to his. Could Richard have been the one that hit Jessica the night of her incident as she rode her bike down the road, leaving her for dead, never stopping to get her any medical attention? Jessica immediately ran out of the house as Richard ran behind her. Richard apologized to her as he explained to Jessica that just as she didn't know that he was the one that hit her, he also didn't know that she was the one that he was accused of hitting in the accident. Richard told her he never even knew he had hit anyone on the night in question. Richard begged her for her forgiveness and not to end their relationship. Richard did not want her to leave without letting her know how sorry he was for the incident. Richard told her how much he loved and wanted to spend the rest of his life with her.

Richard told Jessica that she completed his life and that she was the missing puzzle piece in his life. Jessica thinks that Richard has befriended her on purpose because he felt guilty for his role in the accident. Richard contends that he had no idea that she was the victim of his hit-and-run. Richard tells Jessica how much he loves her and wishes he could go back in time and change things. Richard told Jessica that he was not concerned with his punishment because he earned whatever he got. However, he does not want to lose her or see her in any more pain. Jessica requested to have no contact with Richard before the court date to think about things. Richard could not get her out of his mind. He longed to be near her, to be in her presence. Life without her was meaningless. She had given new meaning to his life, and he had a reason to live again.

They arrived and sat together on the date of the court hearing. Jessica asked the court to give Richard a second chance. She stated that Richard had helped her get back on her feet, and he was truly sorry for his actions. He has since changed his life for the better, and he is now going through drug rehabilitation and has been sober for three years. Richard is active in his church, where he plays the drums, and in the community, where he has started a little league football team. Lastly, Jessica shared with the district attorney that Richard has vowed to take care of her for the rest of their lives, and he should not be taken away from his family. She shockingly announces to the court that she and Richard were recently married and are now expecting their first child. The court, after hearing Jessica's testimony, decided upon her recommendation to order Richard to house arrest.

Richard was on house arrest for the first six months, followed by ten years of probation. He never questioned again as to what road he needed to take in life. Richard and Jessica were very active in the church. Richard and Jessica both accepted God as their personal savior and were baptized. Richard's life was forever changed. Just as the gentleman had informed him, his life was much more rewarding than he could have ever imagined. He was very grateful that he had chosen the right road. Richard shares his story with others whenever given the opportunity. He had finally found his calling in life. Richard decided to go back to college. He wanted to help children he began working as a youth counselor. Richard began helping troubled youth in the community and at the local high school.

Richard and Jessica worked at the same school. Jessica became a teacher at the local high school where she taught math. Jessica and Richard had three children, two boys, and one girl. Their youngest son has Richard's personality and acts a lot like Richard in his early years. Richard fears that he is too much like he were as a child. Bradley has since gotten married to his high school sweetheart and works as a substance abuse counselor for a drug rehabilitation center in his town. Robbie is married to Richard's youngest sister, and they have two children. Lastly, the hitchhiker can still be seen standing beside the bridge, wavering his handkerchief occasionally. There have been other accounts of people sharing stories similar to Richard's. This concludes "The Hitch Hiker" In our next short story, you will be introduced to Armel Benjamin, our assistant pastor, the overcomer in "My Past Does Not Define Me."

CHAPTER 5

MY PAST DOES NOT DEFINE ME

This is the life story of our assistant pastor Armel Benjamin. His great-grandparents were the late Mr. and Mrs. Harry and Ester Bernard. The Bernards were Haitian and were citizens of Saint Marc. Harry and Ester got married at the age of sixteen years old and they were madly in love. The Bernards had eight children, and Philip was the youngest. It was always the Bernards' dream to move to the United States. The opportunities that came along with residing in the United States were endless. The Bernards were finally getting the chance to live out their dream. They moved to the United States when Phillip was three years old. The family moved to New Orleans.

The family got off to a rocky start; in the beginning, the family was homeless. They lived in a homeless shelter for several months before Harry was offered a job in a local factory. They were finally able to get a home of their very own as Ester was a homemaker. Phillip was very close to his father and had a profound respect for him. He loved and admired his father dearly. His father was his superhero. As things began to look up for the family, tragedy would strike. Harry stopped by the corner store every day after work to pick up snacks for the family. He got off from work at 5:00 pm but could be expected to arrive home around 5:30 pm at the latest 5:35 pm. The family was always eagerly awaiting his arrival. Harry was not only a great husband, but he was also an outstanding family man. He showed Easter what it felt like to be loved and adored.

In his spare time, he spent quality time with his sons teaching them how to be men. He taught them the daily necessities of life, such as fishing, hunting, and skilled trades. Harry's family was fond of him and thought the world of him for the unconditional love he always showed them. Harry arrived home daily at 5:30 p.m. Phillip brought it to Ester's attention that it was now 5:45 pm, and Harry still had not come home, nor had he called. Ester immediately began worrying because she knew it wasn't a normal pattern for Harry. Harry believed in being on time regardless of where he was going. He preferred arriving at an event early and waiting for his party than arriving late. Being late was something that he frowned upon. He felt that being late was a person's way of showing that they lacked professionalism and were not interested in the task at hand, coming off as being rude.

Ester looked back at the time, and it was now 6:30 pm. She knew that something was terribly wrong, and she got a knot in the pit of her stomach. Ester decided not to wait any longer. She gave the children their dinner, with Philip refusing to eat, stating that he was waiting to eat with his father. It was soon 7:00 pm, and Ester had the children prepare for their baths. There was still no sign of Harry at 7:30 pm. Ester got a knock on the door. Upon opening the door, she was greeted by a police officer and two workers from the factory. They asked her if she were Mrs. Bernard and if they could please come into speak with her. Ester asks if something had happened to Harry as one of the men drops his head. Ester asks what has happened to her husband and where is her husband. Phillip and one of his brothers hide around the corner listening.

The gentleman tells Ester that he is Harry's boss at the plant and

a terrible incident has occurred. He explains to Ester that a steel metal

pipe had fallen from one of the construction sites striking Harry as he

stood underneath. Ester drops to her knees as she sits sobbing on the

floor. He apologizes to Ester telling her that the plant would do

everything possible to help her and her family during their time of

bereavement. Phillip begins yelling No, no as he sobs as his brother,

who is also heartbroken, tries to comfort him. The company paid for

Harry's funeral and gave Ester a settlement to help with her finances.

After Phillip's father's death at the age of 38, he felt as if he had lost a

large part of his life. Ester was afraid of being alone because she and

Harry had been together since the age of sixteen years old. He was not

only her lover but her best friend.

Ester depended on Harry because she had never worked. Ester was now forced to provide for and make decisions on behalf of the family. Ester's first major decision was where and how she would lay the love of her life to rest. Ester and Harry weren't natives of New Orleans, so she decided to have Harry buried in their native homeland of Saint Marc. Ester didn't want Harry's dying to be in vain. Ester then decided to return to New Orleans to pick up the pieces working on the life she and Harry were trying to build. The company, as promised, paid for Harry's funeral in full and accommodated the family with travel arrangements. Ester was also given a large sum of money from Harry's death that she could live on comfortably for the rest of her life if used properly. A year would pass before Ester met another man getting married against her family's wishes.

Phillip was upset by her decision to remarry. Before the wedding, Phillip and his siblings had only met their new stepfather twice. Phillip had a very strong bond with his father. He loved and admired his dad, wondering how could his mother had moved on so soon after his father's death. Phillip not only felt as if he had lost his father but now felt as if he had also lost his mother. After getting married, Ester and her new husband relocated the family to Chicago, Illinois. Ester's husband was originally from the Chicago area. Ester's new husband was now fifteen years younger than her. He was nothing like Harry; in fact, he was the total opposite of Harry. After moving to Chicago, things would change for Ester. In the third year of their marriage, he began staying out all night and entertaining other women.

He refused to work, spending Ester's inheritance from her late husband to wine and dine his lady friends. He would soon take all of Ester's money running off with an ex-girlfriend. Ester was devastated and yet found herself alone again, and this time dealing with heartbreak of a different kind. Ester was forced to take a job to be able to provide for her and her children. Ester got a job working for the local elementary school as she worked in the kitchen, preparing meals. Phillip, now a teenager, began acting out. He started getting in trouble in the neighborhood and hanging out with rival gang members. He sought his mother's attention, which worked briefly but would later backfire on him. Ester tried to find ways to help Phillip as he continued to act out, she decided to send him to Job Corps.

Job Corp is the most extensive free residential education and job training program for youth adults ages sixteen to twenty-four years of age. In Job Corp, it connects the youth with the skills and education they need to obtain a career. Phillip was unable to complete the program before he would get into some trouble and ended up in jail for shoplifting. While in the county jail, he befriended a pimp named James, who was a few years older than Phillip. James was a regular in the county jail. The jailers had remembered his personal information, such as his social security and inmate numbers. After being released from the county jail, Phillip was invited to hang out with James and his prostitutes. Phillip began visiting James and "his girls," as James referred to them regularly.

One day during Phillip's visit, James was confronted by a man who stated that James had drugged and pimped his sister when a fight broke out between the two men. The man pulled a gun on James, shooting him in the chest. James lay as he struggled to breathe as he waited for emergency crews. He died in Phillip's arms. Prior to taking his last breath, he made Phillip promise that he would oversee the operation of his Brownstone. He referred to the home that he used for prostituting "his girls" as The Brownstone. Phillip wondered if he had made a mistake agreeing to oversee the operation of The Brownstone. He knew that if his father knew the type of work he was doing to make a living, his father would be displeased with him. Phillip's father had made an honest living and wanted the same for his children.

Phillip felt the job was by far the easiest job that he has ever had while making a decent salary. He liked the fast money that came along with pimping. The more money "the girls" made, the more he wanted. Phillip would soon begin conducting drug transactions at The Brownstone. Phillip preyed on young girls who were homeless and didn't have families. Phillip was introduced to Emily, a young girl who had recently moved to the area from Boston, Massachusetts, by one of his prostitutes who went to school with Emily. Emily was a college student, and she was new in town. It was her first time being away from her family. Emily was very young and naïve and thought that everyone was her friend. Phillip was very charming and knew all the right things to say. He wined and dined Emily and her roommate before talking them into attending a party at The Brownstone.

Reluctantly they attended the party. They had a wonderful time at the party and decided to attend another party in which they would not have such a great time. They were invited to attend a second party at The Brownstone. Their lives would forever be changed when both girls were drugged at the party. Emily woke up the following day in bed with Phillip and her friend in bed with an unknown stranger. The girls were upset; they felt that their trust had been betrayed. Emily tried desperately to move forward with her life, but she found herself longing for the high that she got the night of the party. She confronted Phillip about drugging her the night of the party to take advantage of her. Phillip didn't' deny his involvement in her being drugged. Phillip told Emily that he was only trying to show her a good time.

Emily began using drugs recreational she enjoyed the feeling that she got developing an addiction to the drug. Emily and Philip would later enter a romantic relationship where they became exclusive. It wouldn't be long before Emily would find out that she wasn't the only one that he was dating. She found out that he was having an intimate relationship with more than half of the women in The Brownstone. Phillip was her first true love, and she didn't know how to cope with the heartbreak. She began using drugs heavily. Emily would later drop out of school because she could not focus on school. She found herself getting high daily. Emily would later come to learn after dropping out of school that she was now expecting her first child with Phillip. He was ten years older than her. She hoped that her pregnancy would make Phillip change his lifestyle.

Emily later discovered that she wasn't the only one preparing for a baby with Phillip. Other women in the house were also expecting babies claiming to be his children in some instances; many had already given birth. Emily was upset and contemplated leaving The Brownstone but had nowhere to go. She didn't want her family to see her in that condition. She had everything going for her when she left home; going off to college now, she was about to return home in worst shape than when she left home. Emily gave birth to a healthy baby boy that she named Armel. Emily, as any parent, wanted the very best for her child, but she also now had demons of drug dependency that plagued her. She tried on many instances to move from The Brownstone but always ended up going back.

She depended on Phillip for her drug dependency and to provide a roof over her and their son's heads. Phillip and Emily had a relationship that was anything but ordinary. Emily rented a room in The Brownstone because it was also home to seven different families. Most of the rooms in The Brownstone were occupied by Phillips mistresses, most of which who had kids with him. Many of the children were not only neighbors and friends but were also stepsisters and brothers. Although they saw Phillip, he wasn't there for them. Armel never had a father figure in his life growing up. Like many other children, he knew that Phillip was their father but didn't know him as a person. They had never got the opportunity to spend time with him to get to know him. Phillip was always busy operating The Brownstone and overseeing drug deals on the street corners of Chicago.

Armel's mother's addiction had gotten out of control. She now,
on the other hand, was either too high on drugs or always in and out of
jail which likewise prevented her from spending quality time with him.
The time would soon come when the police would bust The
Brownstone. In the raid, Phillip was arrested and taken into custody for
soliciting prostitution and illegal distribution of drugs in the presence
of minors. While Phillip is incarcerated, The Brownstone gets behind
on its rent, causing it to be foreclosed. The tenants had less than ninety
days to find themselves someplace to go. With Phillip in custody, they
not only had no place to go, but they also had no source of income.
Many of them either didn't have the education or the experience to
obtain a decent job.

Armel's mother, unlike many of them, had made it to college but oftentimes had an altered mental status due to her excessive drug usage. It was difficult for Emily to live independently because she no longer had Phillip to support Armel and herself. Armel and his mother had no place to go, and she had no money for a place to call home. Social Services took Armel from Emily, giving her some time to get herself together. Armel had no place to go. Emily's side of the family wanted nothing to do with Armel. He reminded them of his father, and they disliked Phillip for his role in Emily's addiction. Phillips' side of the family wanted very little, if anything, to do with him as well. They feared he had taken on some of his father's bad habits. They thought that he, too, was a liar, scammer, and manipulator that managed to destroy people's lives and use them for his personal gain.

Armel was taken in by Ester, his grandmother on his father's side, who raised him until her death. After Ester's death, he was shipped from house to house while his parents continued to go in and out of jail. When all else failed, he was placed in foster care. He was adopted into an abusive home at the age of fifteen. He was forced to leave his adoptive parents' home in fear of his safety. Armel lived on the streets of Chicago. Emily was often seen roaming the streets of Chicago strung out on drugs. Although he looked like his father, he had his mother's mannerisms. He genuinely cared for and was concerned for people. However, he was not given the same consideration in return. He was trusting and quick to refer to a person as a friend. While living on the streets, he ran into a guy by the name of JB from the foster home. JB was seven years older than Armel.

JB was now living on his own and decided to take Armel in, giving him a place to live. Unfortunately, JB was now a member of one of the largest rival gangs in the Chicago area. JB talked Armel into becoming a member of the gang. JB taught Armel some survival skills to be able to survive in the streets of Chicago's toughest slum areas. Many of which came naturally for Armel because he was his father's son. He had seen his father scamming, lying, and manipulating people to made a living. He assumed it was the way everyone did business. Although he mastered all skills, he took no pleasure in manipulating or hurting anyone. Although he was in the streets and taught the rules of the streets, there was still something special about him. Although he had been raised in the streets, the streets were not in him. He looked and acted the part when faced with no option.

Armel's biggest problem was that he was a follower and not a leader. He wanted to fit in; he looked for ways to be accepted by others. He constantly looked for ways to please his fellow man, even if it meant risking his happiness. Secretly he was different; he knew that there was something greater in him. He always denied himself, afraid of what others may think. Armel acted the way that he felt others would expect him to act, and he dressed to please others. Armel looked like a strong individual, unwilling to take anything from anyone standing his ground, but deep down, he was the total opposite. Armel had witnessed several acts of gang violence; in many instances, he was even forced to participate in some senseless acts of crime. Although he looked the part, he desperately wanted to leave the life of crime that came along with being in the gang.

He knew that if he left, he would have to pay a hefty price, perhaps even with his very own life. Not to mention he now knew too much about the gangs to ever leave peacefully, and they were the family that he didn't have, many of which were his mentors. JB gave Armel his very first driving lesson in a stolen 1986 Oldsmobile Cutlass with a moon roof candy apple red in color. He even introduced him to his first girlfriend and taught him about sex. JB was the brother that he didn't have growing up. Armel contemplated ways to tell JB that he was leaving the gang. Armel felt that his gang involvement would ultimately land him in jail or, even worse, cost him his life. JB knew that Armel wasn't cut out for the gangs. Armel wasn't capable of harming anyone. Armel himself still acted like a big kid, as expected, because he never really had a childhood. He was forced to grow up extremely fast.

After much debate, Armel decided that he had made up his mind

he was leaving the gang regardless of the consequences of his actions.

One Friday night, Armel decided that he would spend some quality time

with his girlfriend Lynn, utilizing some of the skills that JB taught him,

followed by a night out on the town. Armel and his girlfriend, after

returning from the movies, spotted JB going into the neighborhood

supermarket store. Armel thought, what a perfect time than now to have

a talk with JB about him leaving the gang. Armel entered the store

fifteen minutes after JB had entered the store. Armel enters the store in

the middle of JB, robbing the store. Armel, unaware of what was taking

place, began to yell JB 's name. With his gun drawn on the store's

owner, JB turns to look at Armel. The store owner fires his gun, striking

JB in the abdomen.

Ricky, another member of their gang who had taken cover in the back of the store behind a rack, fired back, striking the owner in the head. Armel and Ricky both turned, running out of the store. Armel grabs his girlfriend as the trio jumps into the getaway car. The local television news station constantly broadcasts the videos of both Ricky and Armel. They were asking the public for help in identifying the suspects. Armel discovers that the store owner and JB have died from their injuries. Armel's girlfriend talks him into turning himself in to the police. While Ricky remained on the run. She tells him that there are people, as well as herself, that can verify they were at the movies the night of the incident. Armel and his girlfriend can verify that he had no known knowledge of what was unfolding as he walked into the corner store to speak with JB.

The police is called, and they take both Armel and Lynn into custody for questioning. Armel finds out that JB and Ricky had planned to rob the supermarket. Armel is speechless and doesn't know where to turn for help. Members of the gang blame Armel for JB's death stating that JB was killed because of Armel's interference. Even worse, Armel finds out that JB, who he has known a large portion of his life and always looked at like a big brother was his stepbrother. JB was one of Armel's father's kids, although they had different mothers. Armel learned that JB knew that Armel was his brother. JB, being Armel's brother, explained why he was overly protective of him. The gang, mainly JB, had always been there for him. Now the only family he had actively involved in his life was dead. He had no one when he needed someone the most.

Armel was denied a bond and had to remain in jail until his hearing. Ricky was picked up six months later as he was spotted in Atlanta, Georgia, and he was extradited back to Chicago. The time had finally come for the case to go to trial. Lynn, Armel's girlfriend, testified that Armel was with her on the night in question. She testifies that he only went into the store to talk with JB, not knowing what was taking place. The district attorney had no interest in Lynn's testimony. They wanted to prove that Armel was also a part of the gang. Which wasn't hard to do by his very own testimony. Armel testified on trial that he only went to the store to inform JB that he no longer wanted to be a member of the gang. They knew that Armel's gang had planned and committed the crime.

The district attorney's argument was if Armel was not involved, why did he flee from the scene the night of the murders instead of staying to speak with the police. The district attorney decided to charge him with guilty by association, murder, and withholding information. Armel was asked to take a guilty plea of ten years imprisonment and ten years' probation. Armel refused, stating that he was innocent and had done nothing wrong. He was trialed and found guilty, and he was sentenced to twenty years in prison for failing to accept the guilty plea. Ricky was also sentenced to twenty years in prison. However, went the district attorney heard about Ricky running from police, ten extra years were added to his sentence for a total of thirty years in prison. Due to the crowding of the jails, Ricky and Armel were sent to two different prisons to carry out their sentence.

While in prison, Armel was forced to grow up. He now had to be a man and think for himself. In prison, he had to make many choices that were decided upon by him and only him. Armel was in constant fear for his life. He could no longer turn to his gang members because they now blamed him for JB's murder. One day on the prison yard, while playing a game of basketball, an inmate from one of the rival gangs recognized Armel as a member of the opposing gang and attempted to stab him. The perpetrator was taken down before he was able to stab Armel. Word of the incident got out as Armel feared for his safety. Armel awoke the following morning to an inmate standing over him. He says to Armel, "That was sure close, my boy; you were almost killed yesterday, I heard." As Armel sits up in the bed and looks at him closely, he realizes it is Phillip, his father.

Armel was happy to see a familiar face because he had not seen Phillip in years, nor did he have a close relationship with him. Phillip and Armel spent hours upon hours catching up on the old days. Armel was surprised to know that Phillip knew more about him than he was aware. Armel explained to Phillip the events surrounding his arrest and incarceration. Phillip told Armel that the best way to ensure his safety while in prison was to join one of the organizations. Philip told Armel that he was a part of the Muslin community, and they had a strong bond. Armel made some life-altering decisions. He, too, decided to become a member of the Muslim community. Armel and Phillip now had the opportunity to spend more time together than he ever would have imagined. Phillip had never been there for Armel. He used each opportunity to bond with Armel to compensate for lost times.

Armel had dropped out of school in grade school now he was given a chance to get his diploma. In his spare time, Armel worked on getting his (GED) General Education Development. He not only got his certificate while he was incarcerated, but he also learned a lot about his dad and himself as a person. Armel could always draw, but he never really had time. He had always had so much going on in his daily life. Armel began experimenting with water paint at the advice of his cellmate, who was also an artist. Armel started drawing pictures and paintings made of watercolor for other inmates. He exchanged them for extra food and different items. His paintings came alive on the canvas. He incorporated real-life human images such as synthetic human hair and human clothing. He used things of sentimental value to the individual in which the painting was being created.

Before long, Armel's images began showing up all around the prison. The Warden requested to have Armel brought to him to speak with him. Armel was unsure of why the Warden was requesting to speak with him. When arriving in the Warden's office to talk with him, he notices that the Warden has a visitor. The Warden tells Armel that he had been informed that he was responsible for the paintings that were showing up around the prison. Armel is unsure how he should answer, contemplating what he should say. He answers yes, I am the one that painted the pictures. Armel thinks to himself that now he will be required to remove the pictures, or his sentence may be increased. The gentleman intervenes as he introduces himself to Armel as a member of the governor's office. He tells Armel that the governor was looking for ways to beautify the city and bring positive vibes.

He feels that Armel can help with their efforts. The man tells

Armel that he has noticed several of his paintings during his last two

visits that he finds breathtaking. He tells Armel that they are willing to

pay him a salary for his efforts to help beautify the city and their

neighboring towns. He tells Armel that eighty percent of the money will

go into an escrow account that he may be able to use however he sees

fit once he is released from prison. The remaining twenty percent of the

money would go on a debit card for him to use immediately. Armel

gladly accepts the job; he tells Armel that he will pick him up in the

morning at the gate to begin his first job. Armel felt as if just when he

thought that his life was over, things were starting to look up for him.

Armel and his cellmate were picked up at the front gate the following

morning.

The two men were given supplies and taken to the areas where the painting was to be displayed. They were given a portfolio of pictures that they were allowed to paint. The men would work for hours on their paintings. They were given an hour lunch break where they were allowed to choose from several local restaurants to order their lunch. However, they were not allowed to leave. The men would be gone for most of the day before returning to prison. They would eventually form a bond with Gary, the engineer overseeing the project. He soon entrusted them to paint whatever they wanted to paint, provided it was seen in a positive light. They began taking on projects requiring them to stay overnight, some of which even took them out of town. Armel's mishap, which he considered a curse, had begun to become a blessing for him.

The time had finally come for Armel's cellmate to be released, he had completed his time. Armel began painting by himself. He began attracting not only the attention of the town's people, but he also attracted local contractors' attention. However, there was just one problem he wasn't a free man, which meant that technically he belonged to the state until he completed his jail sentence. Armel and Gary had become the best of friends, and Gary wanted to see Armel flourish in all areas of his life. Gary knew that with Armel being a free man and painting, he would stand to gain much more than he could ever imagine. It would mean a new life and new beginnings for Armel. Gary had never asked Armel about his past until now and what he was accused of to go to prison.

Gary had been working with the government and the prison system for over twenty years, and he was usually a good judge of character. He knew that by the short time that he had spent getting to know Armel that he could not harm a fly, and he was very innocent. After hearing Armel's story, he agreed to hire a group of attorneys to appeal Armel's case. Gary reached out to a close friend who he later hired as the head attorney to oversee Armel's case. Six months later, Armel's case was going back to court. Armel's case was appealed, and it was overturned, and he was released from prison. Armel was also paid by the state for being wrongfully accused in the case. After Armel's trial, upon his return to jail to share his news with his father, he learned that Phillip had passed earlier that morning due to cardiac arrest.

Armel was stricken again by another tragedy, but he was grateful for the opportunity to bond with Phillip before his passing. Armel, after being released from prison, continued to work with Gary. After the completion of the city's beautification project, Armel opened his very own business. He is a contractor for several of the area's businesses. Armel has employed over five hundred workers. Whenever given the opportunity, Armel visits many of the local schools and colleges, sharing his life story. Armel works in the community with many youth groups informing them of the importance of being a leader and not a follower. He also works with at-risk youth, telling them the importance of not getting involved with gangs. Armel would go on to marry Lynn, and they would move away and start their very own family.

Armel and Gary would remain in touch with one another, becoming lifelong friends. Gary was Armel's best man at his wedding and the godparent of his first child. While in prison, Emily has changed her life, rededicating her life back to Christ, and is no longer on drugs. Emily has decided to go back to school, where she will pursue her bachelor's degree in business management. Armel has not met all his siblings; he plans to have a family reunion. In our final short story, you will meet two extraordinary young ladies who happen to be sisters in Christ and the very best of friends. You will read the life stories of Blakeney Riddenburg and Ashlyn and Ace McClain in "The Chosen Ones."

CHAPTER 6

THE CHOSEN ONES

In this story, you will meet Blakeney Riddenburg and her best friend, Ashlyn McClain. Blakeney Riddenburg is the overseer of the church's ministry for disabled members. Blakeney is in charge of transportation services, seating arrangements, and any services to better assist those individuals with disabilities. Ashlyn McClain is the overseer of the youth ministry and the youth choir to include any activities involving the youth. In our final short story, Blakeney Riddenburg and Ashlyn McClain will share their life stories and how they met. Ashlyn is the church's youngest leader. Our story will begin with Blakeney Riddenburg, as it is fitting. Blakeney comes from a long line of wealthy entrepreneurs. Her parents were Mr. and Mrs. Blake and Tina Riddenburg.

The Riddenburgs were well-known in their community. The Riddenburgs not only had professional careers but owned and operated several local businesses. They were the owner and operators of a local seafood restaurant along with several grocery store chains. Tina was an oral and maxillary surgeon, and Blake was a cardiologist. Blakeney was the youngest child. She has an older brother who is fifteen years older than her who is also a doctor. Tina Riddenburg, when giving birth to her first child, had complications. The doctor, who was a student intern, was forced to perform an emergency cesarean section (c-section) to save the baby's life. It is believed the procedure caused an adhesion inside the cavity of her uterus while also damaging her cervix. Tina Riddenburg was told a year later that she would never be able to have kids again.

The Riddenburgs were unable to seek legal action because they agreed to allow the student to assist in the labor and delivery of the infant. Fifteen years later, The Riddenburgs were overjoyed when they learned that they would be giving birth to another child. The Riddenburgs had gotten older, and things had now changed since giving birth to their son. Tina's pregnancy with Blakeney was complicated. Her body had now changed, causing her to have complications with her pregnancy. Tina had pregnancy-related hypertension termed preeclampsia. Preeclampsia is the medical name given when a woman who previously had normal blood pressure suddenly develops high blood pressure. Tina was forced to deliver Blakeney early due to the severity of her preeclampsia. After giving birth to Blakeney, they knew instantly that it was something special about her.

The Riddenburgs would soon learn that Blakeney was born with cerebral palsy. Cerebral palsy is a group of disorders that affect a person's ability to move and maintain balance and posture. Cerebral palsy is one of the more common motor disabilities in children. Many children with milder forms of cerebral palsy have an average survival time similar to those of the general population. Children with mild cerebral palsy have a ninety-nine percent chance of living to twenty years of age. In contrast, according to studies, children with severe cerebral palsy have a forty percent chance of survival. The Riddenburgs, being professionals and well-known, wondered what others would think. They feared that their reputation would be tarnished.

The Riddenburgs were much too proud to have their family name associated with anyone (including their very own child) that would tarnish the family's name. The Riddenburgs had worked hard to keep the family's name in good standing. Blake Riddenburg's father was a reputable judge, and his mother operated the family's business in their hometown for several years before leaving their legacy for the family to carry on. The Riddenburgs were not just prominent figures but also knew a lot of other prominent figures internationally and globally in the world of entertainment. The Riddenburgs' names alone carried weight because of who they were. They were on numerous committees and oversaw many of the town's events. They felt that Blakeney's disability would destroy their image. They were embarrassed by her disability.

The Riddenburgs kept Blakeney out of the public's eye until they could no longer do so. The Riddenburgs then decided to place Blakeney, at four years old, into a group home that was a long-term care facility. Blakeney was raised in a group home for medically disadvantaged children. The home was for individuals with disabilities and illnesses that required long-term care. The facility was designed to aid its clients with gaining their independence. There were doctors and nurses that were on call twenty-four hours a day. The Riddenburgs visited Blakeney on the holidays and special occasions such as her birthday. The Riddenburgs went to great lengths to keep Blakeney's identity concealed. Many of their closest friends and even some relatives never knew of Blakeney's existence.

The group home took in children, in most instances, that had no family or had no place to go and needed ongoing medical treatment of some sort. In the group home, the children were taken to church and encouraged to participate in community service. Blakeney enjoyed attending church services and looked forward to taking part in community service. Blakeney enjoyed being around her group home family as well as her church family. They didn't look at her as a disabled individual, but they looked at her as the loving person she was. Before coming to the medical facility, Blakeney could not speak and had problems walking and standing on her own. Blakeney, with the help of medical specialists and her determination, had made a lot of progress. Blakeney refused to allow her disability to get in the way. She wanted to be viewed as an ordinary teenager.

Blakeney did not allow her disability to define her, but she interned defined her disability. Blakeney lived a regular life despite her battle with her disability. She lived life to the fullest and encouraged others to do the same. Blakeney hated when she was singled out and treated differently. Blakeney went to school and worked a part-time job while in school. Over the summer, she went to work full-time. Blakeney enrolled in a driving course where she took driving lessons to get her driver's permit. She was the first in her group of friends to get her driver's license. Fourteen hours away, in Nashville, Tennessee, you will meet the McClain family. Ace McClain, a native of Nashville, he is a country music singer that was recognized and nominated for several accolades to include the Academy of Country Music (CMA), Country Music Association (CMA), and American Country Music (ACM).

Ace came from a family that had a musical background, and as a result, it was second nature to him. Ace McClain was the son of the legendary Louis McClain. Louis McClain was listed in the Country Music Hall of Fame. He was one of the best country music artists in the history of country music. Ace's childhood dream was to follow in his father's footsteps, hoping to become as great a musician as his father. Ace knew he was destined to make music. His love for music was undeniable, and it showed in his performances. He was an outstanding performer, and he had millions of fans. Ace was born to perform. He felt at home on stage; it was his comfort zone. Ace sang with style and grace. He was a natural. Ace was finally able to live out his dream as a country music artist. He traveled the world doing what he enjoyed most while making a very impressive salary.

Ace's career as a musician was enriching because he was accredited with changing many people's lives. However, there were times when he received negative backlash when things weren't done the way others felt they should have been done, resulting in some undesirable drawbacks. Ace began performing at an early age and, as a result, endured some hardships early on in his career. Ace and his band had experienced some run-ins with the law and had many wild nights on the road. They had delt with some wild women that nearly costed some of them their families and, in some cases, caused other members of the band their freedom. However, it was all behind them now. Ace had hired a few new members, and the original members that were still with the group were now older and wiser. Ace and his group were excited to get back on stage to share their new music with their fans.

Things were finally looking up for them. Ace had been planning his comeback tour for five years, and now the time had finally come for them to put their plan into motion. The McClains, Ace and Mandy-Lynn, his wife of seventeen years, planned to surprise their daughter Ashlyn with a sweet sixteen birthday party. At Ashlyn's sweet sixteen birthday party, she would receive a 2023 McLaren Artura sports car, white in color with specks of silver with pink trimmings and pink interior. The car's plates had Ashlyn's name imprinted on her plates and had her initials engraved into the headrest of the seats. The party was a success as planned, everyone and especially Ashlyn had a wonderful time at the party. At the conclusion of the party Ace and his crew would all leave the party heading to the airport.

As the group boarded their flight to Paris, preparing for their worldwide tour, tragedy struck. It wouldn't be long before Ace would get a call from his manager. Ace's manager informed him that there had been an incident involving Ashlyn and he needed to get home as soon as possible. On the group's way back to Nashville Ace got a call from his public relations representative telling him to tune in to world-wide news. They immediately saw the news feed that read breaking news "Ashlyn McClain Daughter of Country Music Legend Ace McClain Clings to Life" following an overnight incident. The announcer informs viewers that he will provide more details of the story as it becomes available. The group is speechless as Ace fears for Ashlyn's life. Ace reaches out to his wife Mandy-Lynn, as he learns the details surrounding the accident.

Ashlyn was sitting in her car at the red light when a drunken driver turning at a high rate of speed overcorrected, striking her vehicle in the side, and turning it over. Ashlyn is airlifted to the hospital, where she is rushed into emergency surgery and placed on life support, where she fights for her life. The drunk driver was treated for minor injuries and released, where he was taken into custody. The drunken driver is booked into the jail and denied bond. Ashlyn's family rushes to be by her side. Ace is distraught when he hears the news and blames himself for buying Ashlyn the car for her birthday. Ace not only blamed himself but began to blame God for Ashlyn's incident. Ace began to question God as to why he had allowed Ashlyn's accident to happen. Ace was angry with God and decided that he no longer needed him. Ace not only stopped praying, but he refused to acknowledge him.

Ace would soon experience problems like he could not imagine.

Ace's fan base and supporters would soon have a change of heart, turning on him. A few days later, Ace would awaken to twenty missed calls on his phone's voicemail, all from his publicist. Before Ace was given the opportunity to replay and reply to the messages, he was interrupted by his publicist and his wife. Mandy-Lynn, who stood at the foot of his bed insisting that he tune into the morning news. Ace was surprised to see his fans worldwide gathered in groups trashing and burning his CDs and his memorabilia. Ace looks over to his publicist and inquires as to what happened to prompt such a reaction from his fans. Ace was one of the most beloved country singers of all time. Many artists looked up to Ace because he had an impressive career in the music industry and lived up to his name.

Ace's publicists informed him that she had been trying to call him all morning since the news hit the blogs. The fans were given incorrect information by the media. Perhaps someone reported the incident before getting all of the facts. The fans were told that Ashlyn was the drunken driver and caused the incident. Ace's music sales declined overnight. He went from being number one on Billboard's Chart to not making the Billboard Charts at all. Ace felt as if he was in a horrible nightmare. Ace was served notice that he was being dropped by many of the endorsement companies that he had signed contracts, and his music was being pulled from internet sites and out of the stores. Ace's record label refused to release his new and upcoming record due to the negative publicity stating that it would not be given a fair chance. Ace's troubles were far from over.

He had lost millions of dollars in revenue for the numerous concerts that were canceled following Ashlyn's incident. Ace was still responsible for paying the vendors and guest artist. He was threatened by concert promoters of being sued if payment wasn't received. Ace was in danger of losing all of his personal possessions he was forced to go on with the concert as planned. Mandy-Lynn was forced to step in to assist with the concert. Although Ace decided to go on with the concert as planned, he was left with no option but to cancel the remainder of the tour. The number of attendees went from one hundred percent to less than thirty percent. Ace wasn't selling enough tickets to cover the cost of his expenses and was forced to end his tour. Meanwhile, Ashlyn is still hospitalized, and she is in a drug-induced coma to aid with her pain. Ace feared losing Ashlyn.

Ace begins to rethink his very own life. Although Ace was reared in a Christian household and taught about God early on, he had not been to church in years. Ace goes back to God, where he immediately repents from his sin, begs for forgiveness, and accepts God as his personal savior. Ace knew that he needed to rededicate his life back to Christ. Through his fame, he had gotten complacent and felt as if he was doing it all by himself, which simply wasn't the case. He wondered if Ashlyn's accident was God's way of telling them they needed to get back in church, rededicating their lives back to Christ. Ace prayed, asking God that if he spared Ashlyn's life that he and his family would change their lives. Ace's prayer was honored. Ashlyn remained on life support for six months before waking up from a drug-induced coma.

The McClains were told by doctors that she would never be able to live life like a healthy teenager and would require someone to be with her at all times. Ashlyn's doctor tells the McClains that Ashlyn has a long road to recovery. She has to learn how to walk and talk again. The McClains were in need of help to properly care for her. Ashlyn needed therapy to successfully return to her life as she once knew it. Ashlyn is temporarily placed into a group home for medically disabled individuals following the completion of her therapy. The treatment center works to assist her in getting the treatment she needs to return to her daily life. Ashlyn is roommates with Blakeney. Ashlyn is experiencing depression as she lays in her bed staring out of her room window daily. Ashlyn can be seen jumping in her sleep as she reflects back on the incident that nearly took her life.

She missed her parents and her life as she once knew it before the accident. Blakeney befriended Ashlyn and started working with her to restore her independence. Blakeney loved the Lord, and it showed not only in her daily life but how she treated people. Every chance she got; she shared the goodness of the Lord with others. Blakeney invited Ashlyn to attend church services with her because she knew how attending church services helped her, and she wanted to help Ashlyn as well. Ashlyn, now a teenager, had not been to church since she was a toddler. Declined Blakeney's offer to attend church services. Ashlyn now suffered from severe seizures due to the head trauma that she received in the incident. Ashlyn was afraid to go out, never knowing when or where she may encounter a seizure. The seizures were not only unpredictable, but they frightened and embarrassed her.

Ashlyn feared possibly having an attack while she was in church. Blakeney, being Ashlyn's roommate, was taught what to do in the event Ashlyn had a seizure, and she was unable to get immediate assistance. Ashlyn would soon begin going to church with Blakeney, fearing being left alone in their room. It wouldn't be long before Ashlyn would become a member of Blakeney's church. Ashlyn, just like Blakeney, found a sense of belonging and was excited about attending church. Ashlyn was grateful to Blakeney for inviting her and desired to be no place else. Like her friend Blakeney, Ashlyn soon became involved in the church, where she would soon begin working with the youth. Ashlyn had an undeniable love for children, and it showed in her actions. She became the overseer of the children's ministry. She began to organize and set up programs for the youth and young adults.

She also worked extensively with the children's choir. The children respected and admired Ashlyn. The time had finally come for Ashlyn's case to go to court. Two years would go by before the case goes to court. Ace is outraged when he learns that the drunken driver, who had a repeated history of driving while under the influence of (DUI), has been released from jail. Ace questions how could he be released back out into society to continue terrorizing motorists. Ace fought to have the case tried in another district when he learned that the accuser's brother was the Chief of police and had many friends in the district where the case would be heard. Ace's request was denied. On the day of the court hearing, the court received a request to postpone the trial due to other findings that could possibly impact the case.

Another year would go by before the case would be placed back on the court's calendar. At the second hearing, the drunken driver pleads guilty and is sentenced to one year in prison and one-year probation. The court counted the time the drunk driver spent sitting in jail waiting to go to court as his time served. He was left with one year of probation.

Ace was at a loss for words. He felt the system had failed them. He no longer had the same little girl that he once had before the incident. Ashlyn wasn't the same loving bubbly, carefree young girl she was before her incident. Ashlyn constantly suffered from nightmares and was often depressed and withdrawn. He felt that justice had not been served and fought to get an appeal. The McClains knew that Ashlyn would never be the same again and would always need assistance and could not be left alone. Ashlyn suffered from severe seizures.

Ashlyn's incident also affected her family. Ace experienced a major setback in his career because of the incident. Ace had made the mistake before of thinking that he could do things without God. He reaped the consequences of his actions. He no longer wanted to make the same mistake again. Ace knew what God was capable of doing he had proven himself to Ace time and time again. It was through God's grace and mercy that Ashlyn had survived her horrific accident. Ace didn't know God's plan for his family and his life, but he trusted the process. Ace, being raised in a Christian home, knew better than anyone how God had fought his battles not on one but on several occasions. Ace pleaded with the courts for an appeal. He knew that his daughter's life would never be the same because of someone else's irresponsible decision to drink and drive.

Ace knew that things are always done for the best. Ace could not understand the reasoning behind his daughter's incident. It was hard for him to see the positive aspects of the incident because the negatives seemed to outweigh the positives. Ashlyn was very grateful to Blakeney for helping her, and they would become the best of friends. Ashlyn and Blakeney inspired one another. Blakeney met Ashlyn's family and was welcomed with open arms. They embraced and thanked her for helping Ashlyn. Blakeney desired to have a close bond with her family as the McClains. The McClains, regardless of Blakeney's disability, accepted and welcomed her. Blakeney was treated like she was a part of the family. She, too, was invited to many of the McClains' family gatherings. The McClains looked for ways to show Blakeney their appreciation.

Ashlyn told Ace how Blakeney had grown up listening to country music and how she was a country music fan. The truth had been finally revealed about Ashlyn's accident. Ace's fans no longer blamed Ashlyn for the incident. Ace's record company decided to release his new music. Ace's record sales skyrocketed. Ace's record sales surpassed his sales from the past years due to the publicity that surrounded him. Fans old and new wanted to hear what Ace McClain had to say. Ace got his original endorsements along with extra endorsements. Ace and his group received an invitation to attend the Country Music Association Awards (CMA). He learned that his new song had been nominated for Best Album of the Year. He knew that they had all faced many trials throughout the year. Ace decided what better way to show his appreciation than inviting Blakeney and Ashlyn to the award ceremony.

The McClains surprised the girls with front-row seats and backstage passes to the Country Music Association Awards (CMA). After finding out the news, Blakeney was very excited. She phoned her parents to inform them of her good news. She got her mother's voicemail, where she left a message. Ace's aids took the girls shopping for outfits for the show. The girls were escorted into the event, where they sat front row with Ace and his group. The group was nominated for and won the Best Album of the Year. Ace and his group go up on the stage to receive their award. Each of the group members speaks briefly, passing the microphone to Ace. Ace begins his speech by giving thanks to God for taking them through another challenging year and saving his daughter's life. Ace then shows his gratitude to Blakeney for being such a wonderful friend to his daughter.

The crowd begins to cheer and show their support for Ashlyn. Ace decides to have Ashlyn and Blakeney escorted up on stage to introduce them to the crowd so that Ashlyn can personally thank them. The crowd cheers as the girls are brought up on the stage. Ashlyn thanked everyone for their prayers and support during the time of her incident. Ashlyn then turns to Blakeney to ask if she wants to say anything to the crowd. Blakeney immediately grabbed the microphone and introduced herself as Blakeney Riddenburg. She shared with the crowd where she was from and stated that she was happy to be there, and she wanted to say hello to her parents, Dr. Blake and Tina Riddenburg of San Antonio, Texas. As they are now out of time, Blakeney passes the microphone back to the stage model as she stands waving and smiling into the cameras.

This concludes Ace's acceptance speech as they accept the award and turn, walking off the stage. Upon Blakeney's return to the personal care facility, she immediately gets a visit from her parents. The Riddenburgs inquired as to how she was able to get into the Country Music Association Awards (CMA) and who had given her permission to go. The Riddenburgs attempted to seek legal action against the Center, stating that they acted negligently. The Center was accused of not putting Blakeney and the Riddenburgs family's best interest at hand, which could have resulted in Blakeney being put in harm's way. In reality, the Riddenburgs were worried about the family's image being tarnished. The Center fought back. The Center stated that Blakeney could now make her own decisions because she was eighteen years old.

The Center also argued that she was also in the company of a consenting adult and provided security. The Riddenburgs were unsure how to proceed because they had been able to control Blakeney's life most of her life. Blakeney was now of age and able to make her own decisions. When confronted by the public with the question as to why the family had hidden Blakeney, the Riddenburgs could not provide a valid answer. The Riddenburgs were asked to give up their seats on several of the town's committees. Many were advocates and had contracts with The National Disability Rights Network. The National Disability Rights Network is the largest provider of legally based advocacy services to people with disabilities in the United States. The Riddenburgs regretted how they treated Blakeney.

They vowed to change how they viewed her and promised to accept her for who she was regardless of her disability. Blakeney was allowed to return to her family's home to be able to live what was considered a normal life. Blakeney was able to further her education. She went to the local community college and graduated, obtaining her degree in dental hygiene. Blakeney got a job in her mother's dental office alongside her. Blake Riddenburg still worried about what others thought about his daughter's disability. Three months later, Blake Riddenburg would suffer a stroke and required therapy to help restore his independence. Blake was placed in the same care facility where Blakeney had resided for much of her life. Tina Riddenburg was able to speak with one of her colleagues to get a medical evaluation set up for Ashlyn.

Tina's colleague decided to take Ashlyn on as a new patient, where Ashlyn would undergo surgery to correct the problem. Ashlyn today can live a carefree life. She no longer has seizures. Blakeney and Ashlyn remained in touch. The girls would not let a week go by without reaching out to one another. Ace was never granted an appeal. A few months later, the drunk driver that hit Ashlyn three years earlier luck would run out. The perpetrator while driving under the influence, struck a telephone pole, killing himself instantly. He is pronounced dead at the scene of the incident. Today Ashlyn has not had a seizure in over five years. Ace, in the beginning, questioned God but he no longer questions. Ace feels it was God's way of bringing Ashlyn and Blakeney together so that Blakeney no longer has to live a life of secrecy.

Ace also feels as if it was also Christ's way of having him and his family rededicate their lives back to him. Blake Riddenburg remained in the personal care facility until his death three months later. Ace McClain continues to travel the world touring. Although Ashlyn has filled in as backup singer for Ace once or twice. Despite her family's rich musical history, Ashlyn has decided to take a different route in life. Ashlyn owns and operates her own animal hospital, where she works as a veterinarian. This concludes our final story, "The Chosen Ones". After the completion of the group sharing their life stories, the group were asked to all join hands. The church's overseer, their minister Ronald, led the group into prayer. This concludes "Ordained Footsteps." In conclusion, many of the events you've encountered in this book were based on real-life scenarios.

Many people, just like the characters in this story, struggle with addiction, depression, and oppression and even contemplates suicide. Just like the characters in the story, we sometimes find ourselves in unforeseen situations. In an attempt to alleviate pain or to fill an empty void in our lives that *only* God himself can fill, bad habits become normal. It is never anyone's intention to become a drug addict. Many drug addicts feel as if they have the power to stop at any time. I believe that many people want to do the right thing but fight the temptations of addiction. My message to anyone who may be struggling with an addiction, depression, or contemplating suicide. Please, know that you are never alone. There are national drug abuse agencies that are open 24 hours a day 7 days a week. You are only alone if you choose to ignore the problem.

In reference to our short story "My Past Does Define Me," Armel Benjamin's mother was a prostitute, and his father was a pimp, but he still was an overcomer despite his background. People put limitations on God and others because a person does not look or act as we think they should, which is simply not the case with God. It doesn't matter where you're from or the struggle that you are presented. It is through God that all things are possible. God has no perspective of persons, and he will use whoever he chooses in the capacity he chooses and doesn't need anyone's permission.

In the story "The Chosen Ones," Blakeney's own family turned their backs on her placing her in a care facility because of her disability. Not knowing that Blakeney was the apple of God's eye and one of his *chosen ones* which is why he made her so special. The will of God is unstoppable. Put God first in all things; he will direct your path. May God continue to bless the hears and doers of his word. To God be the glory.

The End

AUTHOR'S PAGE

My name is DeiAdra NiCole. Although this is an author's page, this is clearly not about me. God is the author, and I can take *no* credit. I am along for the ride on this journey where it will take me only God knows. It is my prayer that this book will be used to uplift and encourage someone. We all face obstacles in life. I too have faced many obstacles along the way. God would not allow me to give up and has proven himself time and time again in my life. In closing, I would like to thank those who supported me. I have just published my third book "The Mystical House." I have three children's books and two adult books that are currently being published. They are all designed to educate and strengthen an individual's daily walk with Christ. As always, thank you for your support. Until next time. Be Blessed!

www.ingramcontent.com/pod-product-compliance
Lightning Source LLC
Chambersburg PA
CBHW041048310726

48978CB00011BA/467